Runaway Creek

Also by Darrel Sparkman

Osage Dawn

Tyler's Road: An Anthology of Western Stories

Spirt Trail Series

Spirit Trail

Night Panther

Coble Bray Series

Hallowed Ground

Hard Times

The Murder Book

The Apocalypse Chronicles

Shepherd's Fire

Blood Justice

Broken Arrow

Shepherd's Sword

Chrysalis

After the Fall

Runaway Creek

A Coble Bray Western Mystery
Book 4

Darrel Sparkman

Runaway Creek
Paperback Edition

Wolfpack Publishing
1707 E. Diana Street
Tampa, FL 33610

www.wolfpackpublishing.com

Paperback ISBN 979-8-89567-468-0
Ebook ISBN 979-8-89567-467-3

Runaway Creek

Chapter One

"We're not going to make it, are we?"

Coble Bray balanced on one leg, the other poised halfway into his pants. Struggling for balance, his startled glance took in Mattie Hurst reclining naked on their bed, covered from the waist down with a thin sheet. Her smile was wistful, showing no recrimination. She was a woman caught short of beauty. Tall and thin, looking gaunt when wearing homemade calico, but that was an illusion destroyed by the absence of clothing.

A storied past left her a crack shot with any kind of firearm. She was also a trained nurse, graduating from an eastern school. A cook capable of running a restaurant that kept people flocking to it at all hours, and a widow with two teenage daughters, one of whom was a savant with a pistol. Mattie was wise in the world's way—too smart for any man to fool.

And Coble? A deputy US Marshal. A man with a knack for catching killers of men, of staring evil in the face and coming away unscathed...mostly. On one side, the judges who wrote the warrants would call him a useful tool, a man ridding society of the dregs of humanity. On the other side? Those that dwell in the shadows? A challenge for some, but most called him a killer. The only distinction between them was the marshal's star and a penchant for righting wrongs.

He and Mattie came away from the destruction of the gambling town of Hard Times with a similar purpose. They had a desire to see if something born of hot sheets and desire could last. Neither had expectations of longevity.

Coble sighed. Giving her a side glance, he could see she watched him with that small, knowing smile. She would wait stubbornly for an answer. Stubbornly, not patiently. Patience was not a virtue she possessed.

With a wry smile, he finished dressing under her watchful gaze. Finally, stomping into his boots, he sat on the edge of the bed. They'd had a good run, but her comment didn't come as a surprise.

They'd met at a creek-side camp where she was fending off the unwanted attention of three men. His intervention was swift and deadly, although he later wondered if she'd needed his help. She and her daughters were still in camp after burying her ne'er-do-well husband. The husband had gambled away their money and then caught a fever he couldn't shake.

Coble often wondered if she had helped him on his journey to the big mystery, but he didn't put his investigative skills to the problem. The husband's gambling would have signed their death warrants if they'd tried to continue their journey.

"I'm sorry you feel that way, Mattie." His hand idly

caressed her linen-covered thigh. "I thought we were working out well."

"Liar." She gently grasped his hand and moved it. "Oh, this part works really well, the physical part." Pulling the edge of the sheet up to cover her breasts, she continued. "In my limited experience, the very best."

He chuckled. "That's a backhanded compliment, if I've ever heard one. My male ego would ask how limited your experience actually is?" With a playful smile, holding her gaze with his own, his hand inched toward her again. She was a lodestone he couldn't seem to ignore.

"We're past the pillow talk and secrets stage, Coble. I loved my husband, you know."

"I know that, but that's an answer to a question not asked." His hand inched closer. "Mattie, you're a woman of high intelligence, with skills beyond most women, or men, today. You can do better than a tired lawman who may come home on his tarnished shield someday."

"My worldly experience will remain a secret." She slapped his hand. "And put your shirt on, so I don't lose my train of thought. This is important."

"I've only known you for a short while, but your losing anything would be a stellar event." He stood, donning his shirt, tucking the tail into his pants. "So, what's buzzing around in that pretty head of yours?"

She paused for a moment before rushing forward. "I'm fond of you, Coble. The girls worship the ground you walk on, much more so than with their father."

"Slow down." Holding up his hand, he said, "I'm

still in a doubting mood. I'm lost here. What's your point?"

Mattie took a deep breath under Coble's approving gaze. "My husband was a weak man. Even at their young age, the girls knew this."

He nodded. "I think that kind of intuition is something females are born with. But it's also been my experience that strong women like malleable men."

She nodded, sitting up and causing the sheet to fall away. "Of course they do...until they get one. Then, choices must be made."

He nodded toward her. "You're a woman offering a wide variety of choices on your menu. Delightful choices. You never disappoint."

She snorted. "Coble Bray, the detective. You never give up, do you?" Pausing a moment, staring at him, she gave him a broad smile. "I don't know what difference any of this makes."

"Are the girls his?"

Her expression sobered. "Now your true opinion of me is coming out. But yes, they are. Although, most married women are guilty of a few very careful dalliances from time to time. Very careful. Especially those with a doting and faithful husband. It's their nature."

Coble nodded. "I believe it. After testifying in a messy divorce, a doctor once told me that less than half the children born of a loving marriage belong to the father of record. I found issue with that, it was a pretty broad brush, but he was adamant. Maybe his experience with the fairer sex was clouded."

He paused for a moment, looking for his hat and gun belt. "Well, you've done it. You've used your womanly wiles to confuse me. What's going on? You have me dealing cards in a game I'm not familiar with. I feel you're trying to tell me something in a roundabout way. That's not like you."

When he glanced at her, tears coursed down her cheeks while she stared at him. "Alright. Straight up. You're not a suitable husband for me. And I'm certainly not what you need. In our brief acquaintance, fidelity has come up in several conversations. It seems to be something you hold dear.

"Oftentimes," she continued. "I think what you want is a saloon girl whose fidelity is impeccable and whose heart is only for you. You're never going to find that."

He met her gaze. "I've never thought of things that way. If true, I'm an ass."

She chuckled. "Don't press me on that one."

Giving him a fearful glance, she asked. "I'm wondering how soon the girls and I have to leave."

"Leave?" He tried to lighten the mood. "Why would you leave? Have you found an itinerant traveler to whet your interest?"

Shaking her head, she said, "Stop making jokes. When you make love to me...no, let's say, lying with me, poking me, whatever you want to call it, you're not always there. Oh, you enjoy it, and make sure I enjoy it, but often your mind is somewhere else. A woman can always tell."

He sighed, knowing guilt was marking his face. "I'm sorry. The distraction is nothing personal."

Her next statement floored him. "I saw the telegram."

The telegram. How many times would his life be

changed by a telegram? Messages on paper. He could make an excellent case for banning paper messages of all kinds. They just caused trouble. This summons, issued by a federal judge in Kansas City, wasn't likely to be a good thing. Especially since he'd already sent in his resignation.

He took her hand forcefully when she tried to withdraw. "I am sorry. You'd think a good woman would be enough to hold my attention."

She chuckled. "A good woman?"

Shrugging, he said, "Exemplary, I'd say. You've never kept secrets from me." He interrupted her reply, "I have a proposition for you."

"That's a strange comment, given that I'm lying naked in your bed." Her left eyebrow rose. "I'd think the need for propositioning has passed."

He paused, making up his solution to the problem as he spoke. "Mattie, you have a home here...you and the girls. Stay as long as you want. I suspect I'll be gone for a bit and need someone to mind the place. That will be an advantage for both of us."

"I thought you retired."

He shrugged. "As you saw, there wasn't much wiggle room in that cable."

She thought for a moment. "The girls do like it here. We can easily raise our own food, with occasional trips to town."

"And you?" He watched her closely. "Do you like it here?"

Sighing, she shrugged. "It could grow on me, depending..."

"On?"

"You. Us. I don't want to be a dalliance available

for when you come home, something to take up your time until you leave again."

"Not even a very careful dalliance?"

"Not with you." Tears formed in her eyes. "I've already mentioned I'm afraid I'll stray. Long, dry spells aren't something I like."

"I can't promise anything more, Mattie. I've found that marriage, or even commitment, is scarce in my line of work. But you're free to live here as long as you want. You're also free to have a life. Living here is no obligation for anything else. No strings.

"Still"—he grinned at her—"an agreement would be nice if an itch needs to be scratched...so to speak. I can't deny the attraction of having you here. You'd be nice to come home to."

"Still," she said, mimicking his phrase, "that's not a long-term solution." She sat up, the sheet falling from her shoulders to her waist...again. With a slight wiggle, she said, "You've had the milk."

Smiling at him, she continued, "And I've known you to be an insatiable drinker. Do you have an interest in buying the cow? I won't even object when you go out back and sit with your ex-wife under the oak tree. Although communing with the dead is frowned on in some circles."

He'd built a bench next to the grave of Maria, his ex-wife. The oak tree the nurseryman sold him was fast-growing. He and his ex-father-in-law often sat and prayed over her and the unborn child. Never together, though. Old Pete still blamed him for his daughter's death, though how he caused a miscarriage with uncontrolled bleeding was beyond him.

"Interest? Absolutely, with no other entanglements." He gave Mattie a regretful shake of his head. "But given the circumstances, let's think about this for a while. I think you're ignoring what I just said. What we want and what we get are seldom the same in this life. Anything else would be a big step, given how little we know of each other. There is no rush, and you and the girls have a home if you want it."

Her shoulders slumped. "Well, then think about it. You'd have my promise, although you'd never know if I broke it."

"Which brings us full circle. I'd know, and then remember how old-fashioned I am."

"How would you know?"

"I would ask."

"And I would never lie to you. Dammit, Coble." She smiled through tears. "For a moment there, I thought I had you."

He nodded, shrugged, and then put on his hat. "Perhaps the city of Lamar would suit you better. I hear they're very progressive over there."

"Alright. We'll be out by—"

He held up his hand. "There's no hurry. I'll be gone for a while."

"The telegram." Her voice was bitter.

Nodding, he shrugged. Some called his worst fault a sense of duty. "Yeah. That."

With shoulders slumped in defeat, she asked. "Where to this time?"

Coble gave her a curious glance. It was hard to tell whether she really cared. "West, I think. I'll pick up warrants in KC."

"You be careful. And I see the way you're looking at me. I do care."

"I'll have help. You should have seen that in the telegram. I'll meet the men in KC."

"Two men? That's different, you usually work alone. Seems odd."

"Odd? The world is odd. I'm just trying to sneak through it with my hide intact." He paused. "Like I said, I'll be gone for a while. And I didn't mean that about moving. You and the girls stay here as long as you want. It's safer."

"Alone, with you not around? That's safe?" Mattie replied sarcastically. "We'll move, thank you very much. It's lonely out here."

He stopped at the doorway, taking one last look. What craziness was in his soul that he would heed the call of duty, leaving behind a woman full of invitation? Something was wrong in his head. If his old friend Priest were still alive, maybe he could make sense of it. Now there was no one.

"Suit yourself then, Mattie. You have a knack for taking care of yourself and the girls."

Chapter Two

THREE YEARS LATER...

THE SMELL OF DEATH PERMEATES YOUR CLOTHES, your hair, and the very air you breathe. It invades your memory, taking permanent residence in places better suited to good times and the scent of flowers on a mountain meadow, or the gentle touch of a woman.

The skeletal remains of waist-high adobe walls and rock foundations of a forgotten and abandoned homestead were far from the mountains. Still, in better times, someone had dreamed here, had worked their bloody fingers to the bone from can-see-to-can't, chasing a dream, only to be beaten by the very land they loved. And the wind. Always the relentless wind. This was Kansas, and she didn't tolerate fools.

A group of men and a couple of women must have thought the crumbling and broken-down adobe walls afforded some protection from the relentless wind and protection from the roving bands of cutthroat renegades and thieves that roamed the area. Their minds, possibly dulled by the constant assault on their senses by wind and dust, and heat beating down on their shoulders, didn't see the walls as a great place for an ambush.

Sharper minds schooled in the craft of murder saw the possibility of a trap and used it well. Wolves wander with purpose to cull the herd of wandering sheep. Unlike wolves, some men kill for the pleasure of it, trying to assuage an unquenchable darkness in their minds. In the aftermath, it was impossible to figure the intent of the winners in this struggle.

US Deputy Marshal Coble Bray walked among the dead, a neckerchief soaked in water from his canteen tied around his nose and face, holding a wanted poster with a likeness drawn of Samuel Laurie, a renegade wanted for murder and the rape of innocent women.

He paused at the description printed on the paper. Only innocent women? The person printing up this wanted poster must have led a sheltered life with the women he knew. But no woman deserved mistreatment, regardless of her profession or proclivities. Innocence was hard to find, but wasn't a requirement, or a measurement he'd want to hold up to anyone... especially himself.

A wheedling voice broke the silence. "Well, is he there? We need to get the hell out of this place. It gives me the willies."

War Eagle Parker was a friend and scout, keeping watch on one side of the clearing. Another scout, String Bean Guiterrez, sat on his horse on a slight rise farther out. Whoever had killed these men was still out there, and would likely have seen the disturbed carrion birds. This was no country to be lax...or lose focus.

"The willies? There aren't any ghosts around here. Besides, it doesn't look like his body is here." Coble shook his head. "Kinda hard to tell. They've been here a day or two, and buzzards love eyeballs and tongues."

"Don't remind me." War Eagle shuddered. "No papers?"

Coble paused a moment, hand on his hips, glaring at his friend. "You want to get in here and help, War Eagle? Maybe turn out some pockets?"

"Nope." The man backed his horse a step. "I'm good right here. It just feels like someone is watching us, that's all. It's making me jittery, and we need to skedaddle."

"Then don't sit there jawing at me. If they are, find them." He gave the man a wry grin. "Of course, you may be right. There may be more ghosts and shadows around here that you can shake a stick at, that's for sure. We could build a haunted house right here and make a fortune."

"Uh," String Bean called. "Dust cloud?"

Coble continued. "Some of these bodies seem older than the others."

"You mean...?"

"Good place for an ambush."

War Eagle waved his hand in front of his face. "Well, not with this smell. Nobody in their right mind would stop here. Not for a long time."

With a disgusted sigh, Coble finally gave it up, trudging back to his horse, footsteps heavy in the dust. They'd come upon these men in the early morning, led to the spot by a spiraling tornado of turkey vultures. A fetid breeze carrying the scent a quarter mile downwind helped pinpoint the location. That, and a coyote or two loping toward the smell.

"There's still a pile of dust headed this way," String Bean called. "I'd say several riders. We need to grab a whole lot of gone." He pointed away from the approaching dust. "I'd say thataway."

String Bean moved his horse off the slight ridge and stopped next to them, holding his nose against the stench. "Who do you think did this? Sioux? Otoe? Lotta tribes around here."

Shaking his head, Coble replied, "Don't think so. Their pockets are all turned out, with no papers or anything lying about. All their guns and ammunition are gone. Horses are gone. They're not scalped or cut up. Hell, even some of their boots are missing. I don't see any anger in all this. If I had to guess, I'd say renegades. Their stripes or pedigree don't matter. Killing these men was just a resupply. It's how they make a living."

"Right, you are." A voice came out of the brush across the adobe walls. "We'll just add your plunder to the rest. Horses and guns bring a good price in Colorado."

War Eagle glared at String Bean. "You're one hell of a lookout, amigo."

"You're one to talk." String Bean moved the leather loop from the hammer of his pistol. "I was worried about that dust cloud."

Four mounted men emerged from the brush and faced them across the tableau of building blocks made of dirt, and bodies returning to it. Three of the men pointed rifles at them, while the man talking held a shiny Schofield revolver. All their weapons looked well taken care of. Bandits always seemed to have the best equipment.

Coble shook his head in wonder. Thank God for talkative bandits. He held up the wanted poster with his left hand, knowing they couldn't see his cross-draw holster hidden by the large saddle horn on his Texas saddle, glancing from it to the man in front. "Judging by this wrinkled piece of paper, I'm thinking you'd be Samuel Laurie, killer of good men and rapist of little girls? I have a warrant for your arrest. You'll come quietly, of course."

"Oh, shit." War Eagle sighed to String Bean. "That'll win them over."

"I can't remember anyone proving that in a court of law," Laurie answered with a grin. "Not that it matters to you. Now, how about you drop those weapons and get down off your horses?"

"Funny thing about that," said Coble. "Did you know the courts really don't want us to bring you in? Especially since they know what you do. They don't want to spend all the time and trouble, not to mention paperwork, just to see you hang. The public lost its appetite for public hangings a long time ago. Your epitaph will be a tiny item in the paper. Way in the back, right next to some Dutchman's pigs for sale. No one will care."

Laurie smirked, the barrel of his heavy pistol pointing at the ground between them. "Judging by all the big words, I'm thinking you'd be Coble Bray, the man-killer hiding behind a marshal's badge? I heard you gave it all up. Got disillusioned and depressed, retired a broken man."

"Oh, insults aside." Coble smiled. "I'm still the killer you've heard about, just not worried about it like I used to be."

"Boss?" String Bean's voice was plaintive. "That dust cloud I mentioned?"

"Alright." Coble nodded, glancing in the direction String Bean had pointed. "One problem at a time."

Laurie's men had them covered with rifles, but seemed careless about it, like they'd already won the battle and were looking forward to the killing. Their confidence stemmed from the bodies littering the ground between the two groups. They probably had a firm belief that no one bucks a stacked deck. Often, people give up their guns, thinking to avoid a fight, with an abounding hope that something, or someone, will intercede to save them, knowing it's pointless to fight with guns pointed at them. Any sane person knows it's sudden death to draw your weapon when you're looking down the barrel of your enemy's gun. Some might consider it a little crazy.

Barely audible, String Bean breathed, "Oh, shit."

Smiling, Coble said, "What about it, Laurie? Do you want this poster? You could frame it. It's a pretty good likeness."

The outlaw snorted, shaking his head. "Why would I...?"

"Well, if you don't want it..." Coble let the paper go. For an instant, all eyes were on the fluttering paper drifting in the wind. Drawing his belly gun, a short-barreled Colt, he shot the distracted Laurie out of the saddle. Joining the crash of gunfire from behind him, he turned his pistol on the other three men. But they were already falling. In seconds, they were dead from bad assumptions and slow reflexes.

War Eagle stood examining a bullet hole in the tail of his vest. "That was the stupidest, most idiotic exercise I ever took part in."

In the silence following the gunplay, String Bean's voice carried. "Uh, boss? Just so you know. That dust cloud just arrived."

Through the smoke from their pistols, Coble saw at least twenty men spread out on the knoll String Bean had just vacated. After a quick once-over, he felt a moment of relief. It was a hunting party, not painted for war. Of course, everyone is an opportunist. These men dressed haphazardly, from breechcloth and leggings to homespun and leather vests. Feathers adorned their headgear, and the only thing common to all of them was their hard-eyed stare. For now, their rifles pointed at the sky as they took in the scene before them. He didn't suppose white men killing each other bothered them at all.

Noting a couple of deer draped across horses, Coble allowed himself a small smile. He addressed the man wearing a suit coat with the sleeves cut off, no shirt, and a shiny, black beaver top hat.

"Running Dog, the great Sioux warrior. I am pleased to know you're still alive. How does your morning go? Love the hat."

Running Dog was a half-breed and known to most people west of Kansas City. His father was a Sioux, and his mother, a Mexican captive. He didn't inherit the good side of either.

This wasn't the first time they'd met.

"Coble Bray. I might have known." The man made

a sweeping gesture toward the dead men. "As always, death follows your trail."

Running Dog continued. "We were hunting on our lands, not expecting any white men to be around, until your noise chased all the animals away. Up to your old tricks, I see."

"Unless something stopped up your nose, you'd know better." Coble pointed behind him. "We shot these four men. Only them."

Coble looked at his friends, both bleeding from minor wounds, and knew they'd not had time to reload. This was not the time to make a bad day worse. He bargained. "We need to be on our way, Running Dog. It would be a favor to me if you'd take care of the belongings of these men. There are far too many horses for us to care for. And their rifles might help you hunt antelope and buffalo."

Running Dog snorted. "White men have chased the buffalo west, and the hunting around here is bad. The antelope are skittish, and we have no desire to eat prairie dogs."

Coble shrugged. "I believe these dead men behind me killed the ones by the adobe wall. All their possessions are gone. There are many horses and rifles stashed somewhere close. Sell them or trade them for money to buy food. I have no use for any of it."

"But Marshal, you misunderstand." Running Dog grinned. "We will have the goods soon enough. And we already have you."

"Good point," said War Eagle.

"Well," Coble said. "You might already have the livestock and plunder, but you don't have us. Besides, killing a federal marshal would get the soldiers chasing you from hell-to-breakfast. You wouldn't have time to stop by your wikiup to see the missus more than once a year."

The man snorted. "Oh, don't get on your high horse. We are not looking for scalps today. And once a year going home is too often. There is nothing in my wikiup but pain in my ears. Every time I visit my wife, I piss fire for weeks."

Running Dog continued, trying not to look pleased. "Will the esteemed deputy marshal give the lowly Sioux warrior a paper stating ownership of the horses? Or at least, a right to sell?" Gesturing at the men behind him, he continued. "It would be hard to explain our newfound riches when someone finds all these bodies."

Coble had almost forgotten that Running Dog had gone to school before returning to the tribes. "I can make that happen. I'll enter this in my report to the judge, and I'll give you a paper. Just be careful where you sell this stuff. Some folks can't read."

After instructing his men to round up all the horses, Running Dog turned to Coble. "Since you haven't tried to shoot me, I'm guessing there's no paper or warrant out with my picture on it?"

"Not that I know of, or care about." Coble shrugged. "Just stay in your neck of the woods and you'll be fine. The esteemed judge mostly has me chasing men who've broken the law back east, and then they run to the great wide-open to escape. There is one thing." He gave the man a hard stare. "Keep your poker games to a minimum. Please. Word is getting around, and some might treat you unkindly."

A well-known tactic of Running Dog, often introducing himself as Jonathan Bentley, was to ingratiate himself into a wagon train or band of travelers, playing on their goodwill. He would then get himself invited to a friendly poker game. But that wasn't his only game. While doing this, he'd be looking over everything, estimating defenses and what goods were available. It was a risk versus reward operation. If found to be weak, the band of travelers would receive a visit from local bandits the next night. But a good number of people recognized the man and knew his tactics. They'd still play poker with him, a pistol sitting in plain view—giving fair warning at the end of the game.

The only thing that kept the soldiers from chasing him was that there usually weren't any people hurt. People traveling were supposed to be self-sufficient, not trusting.

LATER, after Running Dog and his band of warriors rode away, all three men feverishly reloaded their weapons.

War Eagle dismounted. Running his hand through his red hair, he said, "Coble, we have got to quit doing this. My hair feels loose on my scalp right now. That was too damn close. If you hadn't known that man—"

"I know," Coble interrupted, raising his hand, trying to wave away the well-worn conversation.

War Eagle persisted, hands on hips. "I'm tired of dodging bullets from every ragtag ne'er-do-well lawbreaker. When there's a warrant from the judge, we don't even get a reward for our trouble. It's getting tedious."

"You could part trail. Go your own way," Coble mentioned with a sly smile.

"Now that's just insulting. We're saddle-partners, have been for three years, and you know it. We don't just"—he waved his hands over his head—"part ways."

Coble grinned. "Sounds like we're married."

"Hey," String Bean said, "if we part ways, do we get half your money like in a divorce? I've heard of that. Plus your house and land?"

"You ain't helping, String Bean."

String Bean snorted and turned away. "Wasn't trying to."

"All I'm saying," War Eagle continued. "You need to think about what we're doing. Where you go, we go, and sometimes I ain't liking the scenery."

"I know." Coble sighed.

"We're all"—War Eagle pointedly emphasized all, waving his hand in a circle—"getting too old for this."

"I know."

"Fine." War Eagle took a deep breath, calming himself. "Well, since you already know everything, you ought to know someone needs to treat that bullet wound on String Bean's ass. And it ain't going to be me. I don't want to go blind."

Coble looked at his other friend, shifting gingerly as he sat on his horse, blood painting the sides of his saddle. "Yeah. I know. String Bean, you better peel off that saddle."

"Not here. Let's ride a bit, ain't like I'm dying." He looked at the adobe walls. "I'm thinking a wound could get infected around here just from the air."

"Up to you. I've got some horse liniment with your name on it. They'll hear you screech clear up to KC."

War Eagle snickered. "When it's time, I'll hold the horses to keep them from running off. I'm betting they'll think a catamount is chasing them."

String Bean guided his horse up the small rise and into fresh air. "Some friends I've got."

"Only friends you got," War Eagle quipped.

Coble watched his two bickering friends ride ahead of him. They fought, but were closer than brothers, and he knew their sharp eyes would miss nothing on the trail. Well, most everything. There was still the ambush to talk to them about. They'd won against the four men by living with one rule, something he'd heard once.

Speed is fine. Accuracy is everything. War Eagle and String Bean were adept at both. By the time those outlaws had lifted their rifles, they were already taking lead.

Chapter Three

AMID A TANGLE OF SCRUB BRUSH, SUMAC, AND persimmon trees, a ramshackle cabin perched precariously on the muddy bank of Runaway Creek, its porch tilted and sagging. It looked grown from the ground rather than built, with crooked logs stacked without care, and no foundation to keep it from sinking back into the dirt it rose from. Lower timbers were black and soft with rot, the roof sagged in the middle, and river rocks held a rusted tin roof down. Never painted, nor cared for, the gray surface of weathered wood blended into the land, a scar lost in the rough hide of the wilderness.

From a distance, it could have been a painting, a gentle scene of trees showing mottled green and brown at the edge of the clearing, smoke curling into a sky pale as washed linen.

But up close, coarse laughter, the rhythmic thump of bedposts against a wall, and a woman's scream that rose and fell until it thinned into a long, broken whimper shattered nature's serene calmness. Afterward came a silence so complete it made the creek, burbling over limestone rock, seem loud.

Joseph Thibodeaux stepped through the doorway, the sound of the screen's hinges whining like a wounded thing. He paused, pulling up the suspenders on his homespun pants, his shirt half-buttoned, collar damp with sweat. His dark hair clung to his temples, and when he took in the air, it carried the smells of blood and coffee and smoke.

He squinted toward the fire pit beyond the porch, where a handful of men lounged. There were four of them, all rough and filthy as the cabin. The fire was too big, the smoke thick and white from wet wood. He clicked his tongue in irritation.

"I told you to find dry wood for this fire," he said. "Everyone within a country mile can see and smell this."

A man sitting propped against a stump stirred. "Hell, that's not a worry," he said lazily. "If someone shows up, we kill 'em."

It was Scottie, long-limbed, scarred across one cheek, with eyes that never quite looked at the same thing twice. A bad seed even among evil men.

He jabbed a thumb toward the cabin. "We been waitin' a while, Tibby. You leave anything for the rest of us?"

Joseph stared at him, saying nothing. They hadn't been together long. If the man knew his history, he'd keep his mouth shut. But then, they were all new to this part of the country, and none knew his history—a history of violent parents who became afraid of the only child they'd raised. He fulfilled their fears when he killed them.

The fire crackled and spat between them. He weighed Scottie's tone, the insolence in it, and the twitch in his fingers that always made him look half-ready to draw. Joseph considered the cost of killing him right there. He wondered what it'd do to the others, whether fear would bind them tighter or split them clean apart.

He needed men who didn't hesitate to kill, needed hands to rob wagons and slit throats. Leaving a witness was an invitation to a hanging, so they left none behind. But he also knew what happened when fear turned inward. Men like Scottie got bold.

Finally, he said, "Yeah. Y'all go ahead, Scottie. Might be some blood, but she's got some life left in her."

The men laughed, low and hungry. One spat in the dirt, another adjusted his belt buckle.

Scottie smirked. "As long as she's still warm, that's all this bunch cares about."

Joseph turned his head slightly toward him, eyes flat. "When you're through, dump her in that sinkhole down by the creek."

"Think that's wise?" Scottie asked. "That thing stinks like hell when the wind stops blowing."

"You aren't paid to think," Joseph said, his hand settling on the butt of his pistol. "None of you are."

The others fell silent, watching the struggle for power. Somewhere in the trees, a crow shrieked and then went still.

Scottie blinked first. "You're the boss."

Joseph took a sip of coffee, grimacing at the bitterness. "We'll keep raiding those immigrant trains and sodbusters for now. That's easy money. Half of 'em don't even have guns, and believe God's watching out for 'em."

A couple of the men chuckled at that. One, a red-haired boy no older than twenty, murmured, "Maybe He will."

Joseph's eyes flicked to him. "You're in the wrong business to get religion, boy."

The boy dropped his gaze, cheeks reddening under the grime.

Joseph tossed the dregs of his coffee into the fire, the hiss sharp in the still air. "Nobody can accuse us of killing anyone if there are no bodies. That sinkhole's deep."

Scottie grunted. "You sure about that? The last one, that fella from the wagon—his hand's still stickin' out. I seen it when the mud dried."

"Then you go dig him deeper," Joseph said. "You want to question me, you do it with a gun in your hand. I'm tired of your mouth, Scottie."

"I wouldn't go down there again. That section of ground is shaky, like there's no bottom to it. Reminds me of the quakies in swamp country." The voice faded, watching the staring match between the other two men.

Scottie glared, his jaw working. For a moment, Joseph thought the man might draw, might test how far the boss's calm would stretch. Instead, he spat again, stood, and walked toward the cabin. The door creaked as it swung outward, followed by the sound of boots scuffing and laughter fading into the dark interior.

Joseph stood for a long time, listening. Then he turned to his horse, tied at a nearby post. The animal stamped and tossed its head, uneasy. He rubbed its neck absently. The horse was smarter than most men he'd ridden with, it could sense things, smell the rot in the air.

He bent to tighten the cinch, his jaw set. "When y'all finish up," he said without looking back, "take the wagon and horses over to Mindenmines. Those miners always need things and don't care where they come from. I'll be back here in a week. I've got business to see to."

"Business?" Doyle, the oldest of the bunch, looked up from the fire. "What kinda business keeps you ridin' alone?"

"The kind that doesn't concern you," Joseph said.

Doyle chuckled under his breath. "Thought maybe you were goin' to see that widow up by the Osage. The one with the pretty daughter."

Joseph turned his head just enough for the firelight to touch his eyes. "You got jokes, Doyle?"

Doyle shook his head quickly. "Nope, not even a little bit. Just talkin', boss."

"Then keep your mouth shut. And don't do any drinking unless it's here. You get drunk and open your mouth in some saloon, I'll kill you myself."

He meant it. They all knew it.

He swung into the saddle, leather creaking under his weight, and nudged the horse toward the path leading down to the creek. The animal's hooves made soft sucking sounds in the mud. The night air had turned cooler, with the smell of rain riding the wind from the south.

As the cabin disappeared behind him, he let the reins slacken and looked up through the tangle of trees. The moon hung low and sickly, its reflection quivering in the water. Somewhere out there, men were building homes, raising barns, talking about futures. He couldn't remember the last time he'd thought about anything beyond the next week.

He tried not to see her face, the woman in the cabin he'd just left, the terror in her eyes, telling himself she wasn't his problem. She was just part of the work. Just noise before silence. But the thought stuck anyway, a burr under the skin.

He spat over his shoulder and muttered, "There ain't no saints in this country."

Still, the image followed him, and it was doing it more lately, her hands, small and white even in the dirt, clutching the air as if she could grab hold of mercy.

He rode harder, as if distance could drown it.

Back at the cabin, the men had grown louder. Someone shouted, someone cursed. Scottie's voice rose, laughing, mean and breathless. Doyle kept his head down, feeding the fire, not looking toward the door. The red-haired boy stared into the flames, jaw tight, his face pale.

"We need to cut loose from this, Doyle." The boy's voice was soft.

"Shut up, kid." Doyle looked slowly around them. "You never know who's listening. An outfit like this? The only way out is a bullet."

After a while came the sound of a gunshot—single, sharp, final. The laughter stopped. Then more laughter followed, rough and uncertain, like they weren't sure what they were laughing at anymore.

The boy stood. "You didn't have to kill her."

"She begged for it." Scottie's voice came from the shadows. "You got something to say about it?"

"I just said—"

"You just said too much."

A scuffle, boots scraping, the dull thud of a fist. Doyle didn't look up. "Leave it," he muttered. "It ain't worth killing each other over."

Scottie's breath came fast. "He keeps complaining, it'll be worth it."

The boy's voice shook. "You're all going to hell."

Scottie grinned. "Then we'll see you there."

MILES AWAY, Joseph reached a ridge overlooking the valley. The wind hit him full in the face, carrying the faintest echo of a shot from the cabin. He stopped and listened, though he told himself he didn't care. It didn't matter what they did when he wasn't there.

But he knew better. Every death, every scream, every time a body was tossed into the sinkhole...they were all his, whether or not he pulled the trigger. His name sat behind every order.

He dismounted, crouching beside the creek where the water ran clear over stones. He splashed it on his face, letting it run down his neck. In the water's reflection, he looked older than he remembered, hollow around the eyes, a man carved by things he couldn't wash off.

He thought of the sinkhole, the way it smelled

when the wind shifted, and of the flies that gathered, the way the mud bubbled when it rained. He wondered how long before the ground refused to take any more. He knew the hole was deep, even though it was plugged with mud.

Behind him, the horse nickered softly.

Joseph stood, wiped his face, and muttered to himself, "It's just work. That's all it ever was."

But the creek kept whispering, carrying the sound of distant laughter that wasn't laughter at all.

Joseph reached Mindenmines near dusk.

The road narrowed to ruts between slag heaps, the land stripped raw and smoking from the miners' waste fires. The air stank of sulfur and sweat and something older, something dead. He rode past tents patched with canvas and quilts, past men stooped with picks still in their hands. Lanterns were coming alive one by one, floating points in the dark like fevered stars.

The town wasn't much more than a scatter of buildings—saloon, store, livery, a shack that called itself a bank. The saloon gave off the smell of beer gone sour and the laughter of men who'd forgotten the sound of anything honest. A piano banged out a tune with keys missing, rhythm off.

Joseph dismounted in the alley and tied his horse beside a mule that looked half dead. He stood for a moment, letting his eyes adjust to the lamplight, listening to the hum of the place. Somewhere down the street, a woman was cursing a man by name, a bottle broke, dogs barked.

He pushed through the doors, ducking instinctively under the lintel.

The room was dim and heavy with smoke. A dozen miners leaned on the bar or sprawled at tables, faces gray with dust, eyes bright with liquor. Behind the counter stood Ward, the owner, a tall man with arms like timber and a scar that ran across his jaw. He looked up when Joseph entered.

"Thought you'd be back," Ward said. "Heard you've been working east of here."

Joseph nodded. "Work's work. You got a place we can talk?"

Ward jerked his head toward a small room behind the bar. "Same as always."

Inside, the noise dulled. Warped boards paneled the walls, and a single lantern hung from a nail, throwing thin light across the table. Ward shut the door, leaned against it, and folded his arms.

"So," he said. "What do you bring me this time?"

Joseph untied the canvas roll from his saddlebag and spread it on the table, showing silverware, watches, a handful of coins, and a Bible bound in cracked leather.

"The boys will be here tomorrow with more."

Ward whistled low. "You've been busy."

"People traveling north," Joseph said. "They don't travel back."

Ward ran his finger over the gold locket, pried it open with a thumbnail. Inside was a daguerreotype of a woman and two children. He closed it, tossed it back. "You oughta quit keeping these. Makes a man think too hard."

Joseph said nothing.

Ward counted out coins from a tin box, slid them across the table. "Price is fair. I'll move this through the miners before the week's done." He hesitated. "You look tired, Tibby. You losing sleep?"

"Sleep ain't worth much," Joseph said.

Ward studied him. "You're drinking?"

"Not tonight."

"Then you're thinking too much."

Joseph pocketed the coins. "You ever notice," he said quietly, "how some places hold sound longer than they should? Like the ground don't forget what it hears?"

Ward frowned. "You talking about ghosts?"

"I don't believe in ghosts," Joseph said.

But he did. Or something close enough that was impossible to outrun.

HE RENTED a room above the saloon, a narrow cell with a single window and a bed that smelled of sweat and mold. The rain came after midnight, slow and steady. He lay awake, staring at the ceiling. The sound of boots and laughter below rose through the floorboards. Every so often, he'd think he heard a woman crying beneath the noise, soft and steady, like it was coming from another room.

He turned over, pressing his face to the pillow, but the sound stayed.

When he finally slept, it was a restless sleep full of dreams.

He was back at the cabin. The fire burned low. The walls breathed like lungs. He saw her—the woman—on the floor, hair spread like spilled ink, her eyes wide and glassy. Her lips moved, though no sound came. When he leaned close, she whispered a word he couldn't make out. Then her hand rose, latching onto his throat.

He woke choking for air, sweat cold on his skin. The window was open. Wind stirred the curtain like a ghost's breath. Outside, the street was empty, lanterns guttering.

He stood, crossed to the basin, and splashed water on his face. The reflection that met him was a stranger, eyes rimmed in red, beard untrimmed, jaw hard but hollow beneath. He gripped the sides of the basin until his knuckles whitened.

"You did what you had to," he muttered. "You always do."

But his voice sounded thin, unsteady.

He dressed before dawn and left without paying.

THE ROAD back wound through thick timber, fog clinging to the low ground. The world felt washed clean, but not in a way that comforted. He rode slowly, the creak of the saddle the only sound. Birds flitted across the path, vanishing into the mist.

By midday, he reached the creek. The air there was still, heavy, the water brown from rain. He smelled the sinkhole before he saw it.

Flies rose in a black cloud when he dismounted. He tied the horse and walked closer. The ground was soft and slick. The hole gaped like a wound, steam rising faintly from it. He saw fabric caught in the mud, part of a dress.

His stomach clenched.

He kneeled and picked up the edge of the cloth. It tore away wetly, leaving something pale beneath. He turned his head and spat, the bile bitter in his mouth.

He wasn't sure why he'd come. Curiosity maybe. Or to prove to himself that their sins stayed buried. But the ground here had a will of its own. It kept coughing up what he'd tried to hide.

A sound made him turn—a branch cracking, soft footsteps.

"Didn't figure you'd be back so soon."

"You should have buried her deeper." Tibby's voice was cold. "Why aren't you on your way to Mindenmines?"

Scottie stood a few yards away, rifle slung lazily across his shoulder. His grin was all teeth. "Boys thought maybe you'd run off. Figured we'd split what's left and call it done."

Joseph straightened slowly. "You got a problem with me, Scottie?"

Scottie shrugged. "It ain't a problem if it's solved."

They stood staring, the space between them tight as wire. The flies buzzed louder.

"You kill the boy?" Joseph asked.

"Couldn't help it." Scottie's grin faltered. "He talked too much."

Joseph nodded once. "Figured as much."

"What's it to you? He was soft. You said it yourself, we can't have any witnesses."

Joseph's hand drifted toward his pistol. "He wasn't a witness. He was one of us."

Scottie's eyes narrowed. "You goin' soft now?"

"Maybe," Joseph said. "Maybe I've had enough of watching men turn into dogs."

Scottie lifted his rifle, slow and casual. "Then you're in the wrong line of work, *boss*." The word *boss* was a sneer.

Joseph moved first. The shot cracked through the clearing. Scottie staggered back, rifle slipping from his hand. He fell hard, rolling into the mud near the sinkhole.

He stared up, mouth working soundlessly.

Joseph stepped closer, the smoke curling from his gun. "You had it coming," he said.

Scottie tried to laugh, blood bubbling on his lips. "Ain't...no...difference...between us."

Then he was still.

Joseph looked down at him, then at the hole beside them. For a moment, he thought he saw movement below—white fingers, slow and weak, reaching upward through the mud. He blinked, and it was gone.

He dragged Scottie's body to the edge, pushed it in. The ground swallowed it quickly, the sound like a sigh.

BY THE TIME he saddled up, dusk had returned. He didn't look back. The creek murmured behind him, quiet as a confession.

As he rode north, thunder rolled low across the horizon. He wondered whether Ward would ask questions when he came back. Probably not. Nobody ever asked much out here. Not about the missing, not about the smell from the creek, not about the man who carried ghosts in his saddlebag.

Pinning his star to his vest, Joseph Thibodeaux touched the brim of his hat against the wind and rode on toward Lamar. He had a life there as deputy sheriff to a man whose earthly travels were between his house, the restaurant, and the office. Tibby was left to handle the rest of Barton County. It was the perfect cover. And who knew, he might just go straight someday, and there was a woman there that he'd like to do it with. She didn't know it, but would soon enough.

But he had two roads calling him. One to Mindenmines and one to Lamar. There was death in either, but he'd never met a man who could best him. He didn't know which road he'd take, only that it was long, and that every mile behind him whispered like the dead.

Chapter Four

Coble Bray trudged up the steps of the Federal Building in Kansas City, Missouri. Pausing on the landing before going through the great wooden double-doors, he gazed at the river bottom below. Dust from the stockyards obscured part of the view. With every visit to the area, it seemed the city had doubled in size.

Built on a high bluff overlooking the confluence of the Kansas and Missouri rivers, the courthouse offered a view of the sprawling growth of a booming city, if you liked cities. He did not.

Far below, he could see the new Union Depot, built in 1878, and the new buildings for the meatpacking industry. From the high vantage point, everything looked pristine and unsullied. From closer inspection, he knew that a layer of coal dust and pigeon shit covered the tops of most everything. Constant foot traffic spilling out of the gambling halls and bawdy houses kept the wooden boardwalks clean.

As he watched, twin puffballs of gunpowder

erupted from a group of people below. Probably a dispute over a painted lady or pulling an ace from the top of a boot. Or maybe just nothing at all. Everyone was mad about something these days. Would-be bad men practiced until they looked whiz-bang in front of a mirror and then walked the streets with a chip on their shoulder, looking to prove how bad they were. And mostly they were right. They were usually exceedingly bad with a gun.

Hearing labored breathing behind him, he turned to see War Eagle and String Bean. Both men were diametrical to their names.

If War Eagle's heritage was Indian, the constant washing of generational blankets watered down the mix—and there was a red-headed Irishman hiding behind the woodpile somewhere with a big grin on his face.

And while String Bean was indeed Mexican, he was short and stocky, with the barrel chest and skinny legs of a born horseman.

"I thought you were supposed to wait with the horses?" Coble looked the two men over with a critical eye. Hearing no answer but wheezing, he chuckled. "Y'all are getting old."

Finally catching his breath, War Eagle spoke. "You know damned well we ain't going to let you do this alone. And if your shenanigans cost me a heart attack, I want you to see it up close and personal, so you carry the guilt to your own grave." The man finally straightened and looked around. "If I wanted to be this high off the ground, I'da gone to the Rockies."

Continuing, War Eagle said, "And look at String Bean. How can a brown face turn blue like that?"

String Bean's wheezing answer was a stubby and gnarled middle finger.

Moving into the coldest-looking building he'd ever been in, all polished Carthage marble with a hue of chipped ice and black veins, he supposed it was appropriate. Justice was cold, but often coupled with hot neighbors—revenge and retribution.

He could hear the jingle and stomp of his friends in lockstep behind him. Wearing a star, he got a pass, but he heard the guard at the door inform the duo behind him of the no firearms rule inside the building. Coble didn't hear a body hit the floor, so he surmised they'd just ignored the man. His friends had already gone against his wishes by following him inside. Following orders, or rules for that matter, was never something they were good at.

Passing a cold-looking desk and an equally cold-looking secretary tapping a drumbeat with a pencil on the barren desktop, the men strode into the chambers of Federal Judge MC Stone. To people outside the courthouse, his nickname was McStone. Coble hoped that piece of information wouldn't come leaking from War Eagle's mouth. The time between a thought hitting War Eagle's brain and verbiage was very short.

Nodding to the judge, Coble put a curious gaze on the man standing beside him. "Hello, Tom. What's Kansas City's finest city marshal doing here today?"

Marshal Speers moved around the table with a politician's smile, shaking hands with each of them. "Thought I'd congratulate you on the latest job. I heard that turned messy. And besides, I wouldn't miss this for the world. Although while I'm here, a few words with the boys might be instructional."

String Bean held up a placating hand. "Now, Tom. That whorehouse was on fire before we got there. There are fires every day down by the river. We were just watching the show. Those boys with the new pumper wagon move mighty quick."

"Not the way I heard it," Speers said mildly.

"Enough!" Judge Stone raised his hand, interrupting. "Myra, would you bring in a tray, please?"

After being served whiskey from a crystal decanter, and toasting the good fortune of the day with hail fellow, well met enthusiasm, the men sat.

Coble remained standing, pulling a leather wallet from his pocket and tossing it across the desk. "I'm done, Judge. It's been ten years of thankless jobs, bouncing around the country, and with very little gain from it. I'm officially resigning."

"Coble," the judge said. "We appreciate your service. As you know, deputy marshals get sent by the hundreds to Oklahoma and Indian Territory. Hell, they're hanging a badge on anyone who'll stand still for it these days. But as a special investigator, you're higher up the food chain than a regular deputy marshal. It's a different appointment. We sent you west and north chasing after killers that make the James Gang look like the queen's nanny. It was a job that required discretion and skill, and y'all did it well. You took a lot of evil men off the table. I get it. You're tired. All of you."

The judge picked up the worn-leather badge case and contemplated it for a moment, hefting it like he could tell its history by weight. Finally, he slid it into a desk drawer, pulling out a new leather holder and badge.

"Sorry, Coble. I looked up the papers. Like I said, it's a lifetime appointment. I can't accept your resignation. But I can change it a little."

"What?" Coble shook his head, irritated with the judge, and not for the first time. "I still don't have to honor it. Whatever it is."

Coble looked at the new badge that said Federal Investigator. "I never heard of anything like this."

"Sorry." The judge shrugged with a smile. "You'll have to die to get rid of it, and we all know where your honor lies. You will always be a servant to the badge and what it stands for. I also have deputy badges for your two friends."

Coble shook his head. "Every damned time you give me a paper to serve, somebody shoots at me. No one looks at a warrant and says, oh sure, just let me get my things and I'll be right there."

"Ahem," War Eagle spoke. "They shoot at us."

"I know. Sorry." Coble still didn't pick up the badge. "We're done, Judge. This last time was bad. War Eagle got burned across the hip. Another inch to the inside and he'd be a cripple. And String Bean... well, he couldn't find anything big enough to hide his ass, so his wound was rather delicate. He may have to ride sidesaddle for the rest of his days."

"Hey," String Bean complained. "I'm always ready, and you know it."

Coble turned and looked at his friends before facing the judge. "It's just not worth it anymore."

The judge rubbed his head and gave him a curious look. "So, what are you going to do?"

"We have some money put back. I still have the ranch west of Lamar. Maybe run some horses and cattle. Someplace with a nice porch with rocking chairs."

"I cannot imagine that. You'd be shooting at passers-by for fun within weeks." The judge glanced at Marshal Speers for a moment and then got up and went to a large map mounted on a wall.

"I had a suspicion you were going to do this." He paused. "Maybe because you've tried it for the last three years. Our country, and I, owe you for your service. And not just in money. So, I did a little digging."

War Eagle rolled his eyes. "Oh, here it comes. Beware a politician bearing gifts."

The judge gave him a hard look. "We could still visit the matter of the whorehouse."

"Anyway," the judge continued. "I put the word out a couple of months ago that you might come home."

"And how is Kansas City's fine marshal involved in all this?" Coble gave Speers a skeptical look.

"I can speak for myself, you know," Speers said. "I'm trying to ensure you don't settle in the Kansas City area. My deputies can't handle that."

War Eagle elbowed String Bean with a grin.

"Anyway," the judge continued. "Your ranch is west of Lamar about twenty miles, just this side of the Kansas border. Correct? I've heard it's a nice place in a pleasant area."

"That sounds about right." He gave the judge a wary look.

The judge sighed. "It is. The lady you left it with moved away, and the county took it for taxes."

"What? They can't do that. That's a lot of taxes."

Coble gave him a sharp look. "You say she left? Doesn't sound like her."

"I'll get to that later. The place has just been sitting there and hasn't had time to get run down."

Shaking his head, Coble asked. "How much to buy it back?"

The judge stood with his hands in his pockets. "Oh, it's free and clear."

"Livestock?" String Bean asked.

"Scattered. There was never much. I don't think ranching was Coble's finest calling."

"Not at the top of my list, either," War Eagle muttered.

"I thought Indians loved the outdoors?" Marshal Speers said with a chuckle.

"That does not mean I dream of chasing cows." War Eagle grinned. "I got used to the finer things in life."

Judge Stone sighed. "So, back to the point. I did the paperwork for the place, including water rights. In your name, Coble. It's yours, all paid for, if you want it."

"All legal and tied with a bow?"

"Proper and decreed by the federal court. No taxes due." He grinned. "I even signed your name."

"Sounds too good to be true. I hope my signature was legible, since I was never much of a penman." Coble gave the judge a hard stare. "I'm waiting for the other shoe to drop."

"Well, there are a couple more matters." The judge's voice was hesitant. "Out where the ranch is... there's no county sheriff. Well, there is, but he doesn't get out much."

With shoulders slumped, Coble sighed, thinking of another job being tacked on as a provision of ownership. "And?"

"That area is pretty tame. There's no Indian trouble, and the cattle wars are all out in western Kansas. The immigrant trains pass by east of there, mostly through Lamar."

"Still waiting." Coble and his friends exchanged uneasy glances.

The judge dropped his gaze to the floor for a moment. Sighing, he glanced at the town marshal and then back at Coble and friends.

"Are you stalling?" Coble shook his head. "This deal is not looking very good."

Straightening his back, Judge Stone spoke. "Six months ago, my brother's wife went missing. A few days later, my brother disappeared. There's been no signs of them since. My only conclusion is that they are dead. They had a place a few miles south of yours."

"You sent people to look for them?"

"Of course. We had a patrol of cavalry stop to look around, also the county sheriff investigated."

"Why the marshals? Doesn't sound federal."

"My brother was a deputy marshal, retired."

"And? Judge, begging your pardon, but getting information from you is like pulling teeth."

Tom Speers cleared his throat. "I saw the reports, Coble. They came up empty. Although"—he glanced at the judge—"I'm thinking, in both cases, they'd have to trip over a body to find it."

Coble sighed, shaking his head. The lure of getting his ranch back was strong, but the whole thing was an example of the carrot and the stick.

"If I read this right," Coble said. "You're setting us up on my own ranch, so whoever made them disappear might try the same thing on us?"

The judge gave them a weak smile. "Seems a fair assumption, although y'all are eminently more qualified to deal with it. I'd like some closure about my brother. This seems the best way to get it."

"There is another small matter," the judge continued.

Coble silenced War Eagle's chuckle with a glance.

"You'll need this." The judge abruptly handed back the leather badge holder. "There's been some other murders."

"Murders." Coble shook his head, glancing at Marshal Speers, and then back to the judge. "Murders? As in more than your brother and his wife?"

"There are disappearances in the area, people with no reason to leave." He gave Coble a flat stare.

"Disappeared is a far cry from murder." Coble glanced at his friends and then at the judge. "You could have led with this information. I'm not sure the juice is gonna be worth the squeezins on this one."

"Everything has a price, Coble." The judge gave him a sad glance. "Even retirement."

"I still don't agree. We're retired."

After the trio left, Judge Stone and Tom Speers sat in uncomfortable silence. Finally, the judge poured two more drinks from the decanter.

"You're sitting there frowning at me, Tom."

Tom accepted his glass. "It's not right, Judge. And you know it."

"Why?"

"You're sending them in blind."

"We told them about all we know." The judge waved a dismissive hand. "Coble will figure it out. He knows you don't get something like a ranch for nothing."

"Yeah, that was slick." Tom shook his head. "You just gave him his own ranch."

"Look"—the judge slammed his heavy glass down on the table, causing his secretary to peek into the room—"there are people down there in that country that need to die. I'm sure they're the ones who killed my brother. Coble won't even have to look for them. He draws killers and ne'er-do-wells to him like flies to a cow pile. They'll find him and challenge him—try to run him off. When that happens, he will do what he does best."

"I still don't like it." Tom shook his head and finally shrugged. "I've never seen him work."

"Guns, knives, or fists. Coble is a killing machine. The only way to stop him is to put him down."

"And you don't care if he dies trying to clean up that county?"

"Why should I? He is a tool, only that. A damned fine one, but still an instrument that I point in a certain direction to do a particular task. I think of this as his retirement job."

"Hope it works out," Tom said. "He may just retire, like he said. He strikes me as a good man."

"I'm sure things will work out. It might take a while, but he can't resist a good mystery." The judge sighed and stacked some papers into a neat pile. "So, enough of this. Dinner at that new steakhouse tonight?"

"No, thanks." Tom Speers, town marshal of the largest city in the area, looked at the federal judge like he'd never seen him before, and vowed never to turn his back on the man, professional or otherwise. "I'm not feeling up to it tonight."

"Pity." Judge Stone reached into a humidor and pulled out a cigar. "We should celebrate."

String Bean, the squat Mexican rider, tightened the girth on his paint, whining in a singsong chant. "The country is tame, he said. Everything nice and tidy, he said. Oh, and there's been disappearances, he said. Maybe some murders, he said."

Shaking his head, he continued. "Probably some farmer running around with a bloody pitchfork and burying the bodies for fertilizer."

"Hey, String Bean," War Eagle chimed in. "The judge gave Coble a whole ranch—lock, stock, and barrel. Did we get anything?" He held up empty palms. "Not seeing much."

"He gave me my own ranch...after he stole it from me. Stop complaining." Coble spoke quietly. "He gave you a thousand dollars apiece. Plus, back pay. In gold. That's a pretty good severance for a little scouting and sightseeing around the country."

String Bean snorted. "A little scouting? It's like a damned parade, being chased by Cheyenne and Sioux, all while we're chasing some ragtag outlaw who always seems to have friends chasing us."

"Well, String Bean"—War Eagle cut a glance toward Coble with a grin—"if you'd leave their women alone, they wouldn't chase so hard. You need to court women in houses with a back door...there ain't no way to sneak out from a tepee or hogan."

"Stop. You're making my ears hurt," Coble interrupted, laughing. "Boys, we've been together a long time. I haven't turned my back on you yet. I don't intend to. We're saddle partners. Like you reminded me, we have been for three years."

"Partners? Don't know about that. Didn't see you at the straddle house," String Bean said. "We could have used the help."

"With what?" Coble held up his hand. "Wait. Forget it. Besides," he continued. "I don't want to catch anything I can't pet and put on a leash."

War Eagle choked on the water he was drinking from his canteen.

"There is one thing to consider," Coble said, swinging into the saddle. "All I got was a bunch of buildings and a lot of grass and dirt."

"So?" War Eagle glanced warily at him.

"It's going to take money to buy supplies. We'll have to take a lot with us. There's no telling what that place looks like."

"Of all the..." War Eagle's voice trailed off.

Coble had gone still, his horse a quiet statue, as he sat staring at the courthouse.

Both his friends stayed silent, hands on pistols, sharing glances between the courthouse and Coble. War Eagle finally broke the silence. "You're spooking me here. Do we need to set up camp for the night, boss? Or should we get moving?"

When he didn't respond, War Eagle spoke softly. "You're having one of those visions, ain't ya?"

"Well, hell," String Bean said. "If we ain't going to make it this time, I don't want to know. We'll just play it out to the end."

War Eagle poked Coble with a finger. "So, at the end of the day, in this dream of yours, are we alive or dead?" War Eagle asked.

"Alive." Coble gave a quick nod, took a deep breath, and broke the spell. "I think."

He pointed toward the judge's chambers, embedded in that cold building. "This isn't right, fellas. There's something wrong with this whole deal."

"I always said you were the slow one of the bunch. We knew that from the first word. First thing is—he's a big-city judge. Second thing? He's a politician." War Eagle gave Coble a serious look. "How about we just take the judge's gold and mosey on down to Joplin? That's a booming place. From what I hear, I figure String Bean would wear himself down to a nubbin within a week."

"No." Coble looked at his two friends. "We'll play this straight up. At least for now. We need a place to retire and rest for a while. I figure the ranch is worth some trouble. And trouble is something we are used to."

"For now?"

"Circumstances alter circumstances."

"Yeah, forget I asked," War Eagle said. "That carrot you mentioned. A nice ranch for free?"

String Bean scrunched his head down and finished

the thought. "It's the stick I'm worried about. What a federal judge giveth, he can taketh away."

"Well, look at you," Coble said. "A prophet, all biblical and all."

War Eagle laughed as they maneuvered down the dirt street past buggies and wagons, and more people on foot than they cared to look at. "What do you expect? He goes to the Church of the divine flop house. They call out for deities every hour in those places."

Coble stifled a snort. "Deities?"

"You got to get yourself educated," said War Eagle. "I'm tired of carrying the load around here."

A few minutes later, War Eagle asked. "Will you tell us what was in the vision? Are we all gonna die?"

Coble shook his head. "Kids."

"Kids?" War Eagle rode in silence for a moment. "We talking goats here?"

"No."

People turned their heads at the laughter heard for miles.

Chapter Five

ADELINA MORROW HOOKED HER ARMS UNDER HER father's and half-lifted, half-guided him toward the camp chair set near their cookfire. His breath came ragged, each step an effort. The morning light flickered through the leaves, sharp and gold, and she could see how thin his skin had grown, pale as onion paper over the bones of his wrists.

"Easy now," she murmured, though her voice shook. "You don't have to rush."

Ernest Morrow grunted, his jaw clenched. "Adelina, I can walk by myself."

He pushed off her arm with a tremor of pride. His legs were bone-covered skin under him, trembling with the strain of standing upright. She stayed close in case he fell.

"I'm just trying to help, Pops," she said. "You're down to a bag of bones now. I'm afraid if you fall, you'll break most of them."

He lowered himself into the chair with a long sigh

that sounded halfway between pain and surrender. The wind teased a few white strands of his hair across his forehead. "Let's be honest, girl," he said quietly, "I don't see how I'm ever going to move from this spot. Do you?"

Her throat tightened. She turned away so he wouldn't see the tears welling up. "It's a pleasant spot," she said after a moment. "Beautiful, actually."

And it was—if beauty could still matter. They'd made camp beside a small river lined with trees just coming into their green fullness. Honeysuckle draped the branches like lace. Wild roses crowded the edge of the clearing, their scent sweet and heady against the smell of smoke and horse sweat. The water in the ford chuckled softly over gravel, and far off, a quail called twice, tentative and lonely.

She wanted to hold on to that peace, just for a breath longer.

Ernest followed her gaze toward the river. "I used to think I'd die in town," he said. "Fort Smith. Maybe even in a proper bed."

"You're not dying, Pops."

He smiled faintly, the way men do when they know they're being lied to for kindness' sake.

Once he'd been a police officer—a powerful man, tall and certain, the kind who filled a doorway. He'd worn his uniform proudly and never raised his voice unless it was needed. After a fever took her mother, he'd lasted three months in that house full of echoes before he hitched their wagon, loaded every piece of furniture that meant something, and pointed their horses north. Said Kansas City would be a fresh start, and the land there would help them forget.

But the road had been longer than he'd reckoned, and now every mile seemed to weigh on his chest.

"I don't know how much longer we can stay here," she said. "The horses have eaten nearly everything close by. I don't want to hobble them too far away, someone might steal them."

"So take them out to the next meadow," he said. "Sit with them. Read a book. Knit something."

"I shouldn't leave you alone," she said, brushing a stray strand of hair from her face. "If I'm away, I ought to be hunting. We're nearly out of food."

Her father chuckled weakly. "Like you could skin and dress out whatever you're lucky enough to shoot? I never taught you those things, and I regret it."

"There wasn't any need," she said. "We lived in the city until you decided to pull up stakes and go. You didn't plan for bad luck."

He gave a brief, wry smile.

"We should have loaded more food and less furniture," she added, trying to sound light. She patted his shoulder. "Maybe in a few days you'll feel strong enough to travel again."

He gazed into the fire where the iron kettle hung. "And maybe in a few days..." He trailed off, staring at the coals as if he could read something in them.

A voice cut through the air. "Hello, the camp."

Adelina spun, heart pounding.

Three men rode into the clearing, their horses blowing steam in the cool morning air. The one in front was broad-shouldered, his hat bent and sweat-stained, his face marked by a jagged scar that ran from cheek to neck. The other two looked younger, meaner.

"Looks like we found ourselves some pilgrims," the leader said, grinning.

"What do you want?" Adelina asked, her voice more steady than she felt.

The big man's grin widened. "Now, miss, don't go getting riled. We were just thinking we might join you for a meal. Smells good." He nodded toward the pot over the fire. "After that—well, you're about the prettiest woman I've seen in a long while. I think you can guess the rest."

Laughter rippled from the other two.

Adelina stood tall, putting herself between the men and her father. Her pulse thudded in her ears. "You'll have to leave," she said. "We've barely enough for ourselves."

"Oh, there's plenty here," the man said. "After we're done, there won't be much left for you."

Her father's voice came sharp. "Adelina, move."

She stepped aside just as Ernest raised his pistol.

The three men tensed, spreading out in a shallow line.

"Old man," the leader said, voice low, "you best lay that gun down. You'll die today if you don't."

Ernest's hand was steady, though his breath wasn't. "I already have one foot in the grave. My pistol's out, and you're covered. You'd better leave. I know how to use it."

"And I can use this shotgun," Adelina said, darting to the wagon and hefting the old weapon.

The scarred man's eyes flicked between them, weighing the risk. Then, with a slow nod, he grinned again. "Boys," he said, "they've got a point. We can take this outfit anytime, day or night. Let's be neighborly and give them till then."

The men chuckled as they turned their horses. Before leaving, the leader looked back. "Don't run off. As soon as I tell the boss, we'll come calling."

The clearing fell silent when they were gone.

Ernest's arm dropped, the pistol slipping from his hand to the dirt. His breath came shallow and quick.

"Pops!" Adelina dropped beside him.

He waved her away weakly. "Adelina...throw a saddle on a horse. You must leave this place."

"I won't leave you."

"It's not safe. You know what that man wanted."

"I do," she said, jaw tight. "But their threat was just bluster."

"Don't misjudge that man," he said. "He's pure evil, and we're not prepared to face that. Look at this. I never loaded my gun. Ten years behind a badge, never had to use it."

Her mouth opened and then closed. "I didn't load the shotgun either," she admitted. "But the bluff worked. No one wants to get shot. They're gone."

"For now," he said, eyes distant. "For now."

They sat in silence, the fire crackling softly. The sound of the river carried faintly and low.

At last, she stood. "We need to move. Kansas City's still a long way, but maybe we can find a small town nearby."

"Look for anything like a road or wagon trail that might lead to someone's home." Ernest rubbed his chest, grimaced, and nodded. "Let's not waste daylight."

By the time she hitched the horses, sweat darkened her blouse and streaked the dust on her face. Her father was weak, his breathing shallow. When she helped him climb into the wagon, he barely held himself upright.

Instead of following the creek, the direction the men had gone, she turned away, guiding the horses through open prairie. The sun climbed high, pressing heat against her shoulders.

They traveled slowly. Flies gathered around the horses' ears, and the wagon wheels groaned, making a new trail.

Late in the afternoon, she spotted faint tracks leading west, old wagon prints, half-swallowed by weeds. She followed them, hope tightening her chest.

At the top of a low rise, she saw a ranch house in the distance, gray and square against the horizon.

"Pops," she said, looking back. "I've found a house. Maybe we can stay the night."

He didn't answer. His eyes were closed, his skin waxy.

"Pops?" she whispered, fear prickling her throat.

A shallow breath answered her. Relief washed over her, weak but real.

She drove the team harder.

By the time they reached the house, dusk was creeping in. The place was silent, empty. Paint peeled off the shutters. Grass grew tall around the porch.

She climbed down and knocked. No answer.

"Hello?" she called. "Is anyone here?"

The only reply was the wind moving through the eaves.

She tried the latch. The door stuck, then gave with a groan. Dust floated in the light from the doorway.

Inside, the air was cool and musty. A chair lay on its side. A coffee cup sat on the table, rimmed with mold. In the kitchen, shelves lined with cans—air tights, she remembered her father calling them—and sacks of beans and rice. Mice had chewed holes through them, but she could salvage some.

She leaned against the counter, hands on her hips, breathing hard.

They could stay here a while. Maybe the men wouldn't find them. And just maybe her father could rest long enough to gain his strength again—or, if it came to it, die in peace.

She turned toward the door, listening to the wind sigh across the empty yard.

For the first time in days, she felt the faintest thread of safety.

But as the light faded, she thought she heard something out in the distance, a faint echo of hooves on hard ground.

And just like that, the fear was back.

THE SKY BURNED orange at the edges when Adelina finished unhitching the horses. They blew hard through their nostrils, flanks slick with sweat. She led them behind the house, where tall grass grew in soft waves, and left them to graze. The air was thick and still. No birds sang now, even the insects had quieted.

When she came back around, Ernest hadn't stirred. He lay slumped against the seat of the wagon, his hat tipped over his face, chest rising shallowly. For one long, aching moment, she thought he'd gone. Then, a ragged breath escaped him, faint but steady.

"Pops?"

He stirred. "I'm still here," he whispered. "Don't look so grave."

"I thought..." She stopped, swallowed hard. "Never mind. Let's get you inside."

It took nearly ten minutes to get him from the wagon to the porch. His weight was nothing now, but dead weight all the same, and her arms trembled by the time she lowered him onto the old settee in the main room. He let out a low groan, clutching his chest.

"Easy," she said. "I'll fetch you some water."

The pump out back wheezed and clanked before coughing up a gush of dirty water. After pumping until it was clear, she filled a tin cup and brought it to him. He sipped, then sank back with a faint smile.

"Not bad," he said. "Better than the city pipes ever were."

"Don't talk," she whispered. "You need your strength."

"Sorry." He chuckled. "Strength's long gone, girl."

She busied herself with small things, clearing dust off the table, brushing away mouse droppings, sweeping the worst of the dirt from the floor with an old broom she found propped by the door. She needed movement, something to keep her from thinking. Every creak of the house made her start. Every gust through the trees sounded like hoofbeats.

Outside, dusk gave way to night. A full moon

climbed slowly over the prairie, painting everything silver. She brought in a kerosene lantern and set it by her father's chair.

He watched her silently for a while, his eyes soft but far away. "Your mother would've been proud," he said at last. "You've got her stubborn streak."

"Stubborn is what keeps us alive."

He smiled faintly, glancing toward the window. "That's true enough. You think they'll come?"

Adelina didn't answer right away. The lamp hissed softly. "I don't know. Maybe not. Maybe they were just passing through."

"They didn't seem like travelers."

She hesitated. "Then we'll deal with it when it comes."

He nodded, satisfied, too tired to argue.

LATER, she found a can of beans, pried it open with a knife, and warmed it over the fire she'd coaxed back to life in the rusted stove. She was lucky it was banked with coal instead of wood. The smell filled the small kitchen, sharp and metallic, but comforting all the same. She gave her father the lion's share.

He picked at the food, the spoon rattling against the tin.

"You should eat too," he said.

"I will," she lied.

When he finished, he leaned back, breathing hard. "You should get some rest, Addy."

"I'm not tired."

"You've been running on worry for days. Go on. I'll sit here for a while and listen to the frogs."

She shook her head. "No, sir. I'll keep watch."

"Old habits," he murmured, a ghost of a smile touching his lips. "You're the one sitting guard now."

The words caught her off guard, his quiet pride, the way he said it. She didn't answer.

THE NIGHT STRETCHED LONG and silent, and the house creaked with the wind, the river whispered beyond the trees, and now and then, one of the horses stamped in the grass behind the house. The wind carried the scent of wet earth and the faint sweetness of honeysuckle from the creek.

Adelina sat by the front window, the shotgun resting across her knees. She'd loaded it this time. The shells were old, green with corrosion around the brass, but they'd have to do. Her palms were damp.

Now and then, she glanced back at her father. He'd fallen asleep in the chair, mouth slightly open, one hand clutching the blanket around his shoulders. His breathing rasped like paper against stone.

She thought of the road they'd come down—the endless dust, the days of silence between them, the promise of Kansas City growing smaller each mile. And thought of her mother, of the way she used to sing while washing dishes, and for a moment, the memory was too heavy to bear.

A sound pulled her back.

Hooves. Faint but certain.

She froze, heart thudding. It came from the east,

maybe a hundred yards off, then faded. A pause. Then again, closer. Murmuring voices carried on the slight breeze.

She blew out the lamp, plunging the room into darkness. The fire in the stove had burned low, only a dull orange glow remained. She crouched by the window, peering out through a crack in the shutters.

Nothing moved. The prairie stretched pale and still under the moon.

Minutes passed. Maybe longer. Then...another sound. The creak of saddle leather. A whisper of voices.

She held her breath.

A figure took shape at the edge of the yard, tall, broad-shouldered, a hat pulled low. Two more shadows lingered behind.

Her stomach dropped.

They'd found her.

"Pops," she whispered.

He stirred, blinking awake. "What is it?"

"They're here."

He tried to rise but fell back, chest heaving. "The gun," he rasped. "Use it."

"I will."

The front door groaned suddenly under pressure, someone testing the latch.

Adelina leveled the shotgun, every nerve in her body tight as wire.

A man's voice drifted through the wood, low and almost pleasant. "Evening, miss. We didn't mean to startle you. Figured we might stop by for that supper you promised."

Her throat went dry. "You're not welcome here."

The voice chuckled. "Now, that ain't very neighborly."

A soft scrape followed, the sound of boots shifting on wood. Another voice muttered something she couldn't catch.

"Leave," she said, louder now. "I'll shoot."

Silence.

Then the leader spoke again. "No need for that, sweetheart. We just wanna talk. Maybe your old man's feeling better? Maybe he's ready to be reasonable."

Adelina braced herself. "I'll count to three."

No answer.

"One..."

Stillness.

"Two..."

A thud—something struck the door hard. The hinges groaned.

She fired.

The blast tore through the wood, lighting the room with white flame. The sound echoed out into the night, scattering birds from the trees.

Outside, a curse, then the sharp report of a pistol. Splinters sprayed across her face.

"Addy?" her father shouted, voice breaking.

"I'm fine," she cried. "Stay down."

She crouched low, reloading with shaking hands. Smoke filled the air, thick and bitter.

When she looked out again, the yard was empty. Just moonlight and dust.

Then, a horse whinnied. Hooves pounded. The three figures vanished into the distance, swallowed by the dark.

For a long time, she stayed where she was, the gun still aimed, waiting for another sound.

None came.

At last, she lowered the barrel, her hands trembling. Her father's ragged breathing filled the silence.

"You all right?" he asked hoarsely.

She nodded, though he couldn't see her face in the dark. "They're gone."

"For now."

She sat beside him, both staring into the darkness. The house smelled of gunpowder and fear.

WHEN DAWN CAME, the light was pale and thin. She stepped onto the porch barefoot, her body heavy with exhaustion. The yard was littered with hoofprints. A dark stain marked the edge of the steps. Good, she'd nicked someone.

Adelina stood for a long time, staring east. The prairie stretched quiet and endless. Somewhere out there, the men were riding, angry and hungry for revenge.

They'd be back.

She knew it as surely as she knew her father wouldn't survive another journey.

Adelina gripped the shotgun tighter. Her arms ached, but she didn't care.

It was unknown why this house was vacant. But for now, she'd stay. She'd fight. And when they came again, she'd be ready.

Chapter Six

COBLE LED THEIR SMALL CARAVAN OF TWO WAGONS stuffed full of supplies into the yard between the corrals and the ranch house. Dust hung behind them like yellow smoke, refusing to settle in the still air. It gathered in the creases of shirts, the folds of neckerchiefs, and the corners of eyes already narrowed against the sting.

The big draft horses snorted, their sides damp with sweat, ropes creaking as they shifted against the harness, stamping hooves and tossing their heads in protest. Behind the wagons, the saddle horses trailed wearily, heads low, tails swatting at flies that seemed determined to live forever.

Three days out of Carthage, although some still stubbornly called it Murphysburg, the wagons had moved with slow deliberation, inching their way across the hard-baked plains. A train might have taken them faster, but Coble didn't trust the spur line that ran into Lamar. There were too many stories of unclaimed crates and riders who stepped aboard and soon disappeared. The last thing he needed was for one of their wagons to vanish between stations. If they were going to make a go of it at the ranch, they needed everything on that wagon.

And besides, he didn't like leaving things to someone else's machinery. Out here, the land was old, and it held grudges. You moved through it on your own terms, with purpose and plan, or not at all.

For once, he was grateful for the lack of rain. The hard-packed prairie dirt, sun-cracked and pale as ash, hard as a plate, and the wagon wheels rolled smoothly rather than bogging axle-deep in sucking mud. The grass was brittle, faded green-gold, whispering secrets in the faintest breeze, and the horizon shimmered like heat off iron. It looked close enough to touch, and always just a little farther than it ought to be.

When the last of the dust settled, War Eagle squinted toward the house, shading his eyes with a weathered hand. "Someone was one hell of a carpenter," he said. "Looks like a fine house."

"Well, it wasn't me." Coble reined his horse to a stop, dried grass crunching under hoof. "I bought it this way. Mostly. Made a few improvements here and there."

String Bean, hunched higher than comfort allowed on the front wagon seat, lifted his chin and spat a long arc of brown into the yard. "I saw you go into the office at the last depot we passed. Did you telegraph that marshal in Lamar about the disappearances?" he asked. He continued with a grin, "Not that we're gonna do much about it."

Coble nodded, wiping his brow with a sleeve gone stiff with trail dust. "Actually, I was just looking for an answer to the one I sent from Carthage. He replied that no one's dead, just gone. Disappeared, presumed dead—maybe alive, but no proof of anything. Wouldn't give me names either. The cable said the judge doesn't want folks stirred up. Maybe he's worried about his brother being missing. Maybe something else."

War Eagle chuckled without humor. "That's cutting a line finer than hair on a frog's ass. Not dead, just gone."

"And his brother is a deputy marshal?"

"Used to be. One of thousands. It's not unheard of, you know," Coble said. "You ride long enough on these trails, you find bones. Sometimes you don't even know if they're man or animal. Sun and wind make 'em all look the same in the end."

String Bean fanned the air with his hat, grimacing. "So who all's missing?"

"Well, for sure"—Coble considered—"three men. One of 'em might not count, left after a fight with his wife, might have just got drunk and kept going. Two women. One of those is a teenage girl. All of 'em went out riding. All on horseback. None came back."

"All on horseback," War Eagle echoed. "That's a clue."

"How?" String Bean asked, not bothering to hide his skepticism.

War Eagle grinned crookedly. "Don't know. Sounded important when I said it."

Coble smirked, shaking his head. "You're investigators now, huh?"

"Sure," String Bean said, eyes scanning the eaves of the house. "Deputy investigators. Freelance. No authority that we know of. We're just full of a lot of *we don't care anymore*."

War Eagle tipped his hat down against the glare. "Too bad you threw away that murder book you used to keep. Might have had clues. You did throw that thing away, right?"

He glanced at Coble sidelong. "Right?"

Coble didn't answer right away. "Doesn't matter. I just traded one kind of killer for another, and they all look the same to me. Before I met you boys, I hunted men who killed because something in their heads told them to. After that, it's been men who killed because they could. No remorse either way. Maybe someday someone'll figure out what makes them different. I never could."

String Bean let out a long breath. "Well, don't that just put a cloud on a bright sunny day."

They lapsed into silence. The wind moved through the grass, dry and thin, like someone blowing across the top of a bottle. A crow called once, sharp and solitary, from somewhere past the barn. A faint answer came from the trees along Runaway Creek.

Coble shifted in his saddle, hand dropping absently to rest on the butt of his pistol. It was habit now, a reflex more than a thought. "Enough remembering. Let's earn our keep. We'll clear the house first."

"Clear the...why?" String Bean looked startled.

"Never can tell," Coble said. "Raccoons, possums, feral cats, maybe even skunks." He paused for a moment. "Don't shoot the skunks. Please."

Both men slid from their wagons, boots thudding against the hard ground. Steel whispered as they drew their guns, not with flourish, but with the weary smoothness of men who'd done it too many times before.

"You two didn't see all the tracks in the yard?" Coble asked. "The new horse apples in the corral? Or the fact someone patched that hole in the front door with a board that ain't sun-faded yet?"

"No need," War Eagle muttered. "The area's tame and settled, remember?"

"Tell that to the folks who vanished," String Bean said softly. "You think there's a two-legged skunk inside?"

A silence followed, not a dead one, but the kind that watched you.

War Eagle's face changed, eyes flicking toward the hill behind the house. "Didn't you bury your wife on that rise?"

Coble looked. The split-rail fence was still there, leaning with age. The pin oak had grown several feet, and the grave he had dug for Maria was there, sunken, grass grown over. But now the ground looked wrong. The soil next to Maria's grave was churned up, dark and uneven. Recently disturbed.

"Looks like a fresh grave," War Eagle said quietly.

"It does for a fact," Coble answered, voice low.

He dismounted slowly, boots hitting the ground with a dull thud. The wind tugged at his coat, whispering through the dry grass. Maria. Her name passed through his chest like a bell tolling somewhere deep. He remembered the iron smell of blood, the cold sweat on her brow, her whisper-thin breathing at the end. Strangely, Maria hadn't cried. She'd gone still before the sun came up.

Coble's jaw tightened. "Change of plans. Act like

you're moving the wagons to unload. Once you're close to the porch, come in through the front. We'll deal with the stock later. Any hay in that barn's probably nothing but straw by now."

"Don't teach an old dog how to suck eggs," War Eagle said, re-holstering his pistol. "Let's get it done. I could eat the south end of a northbound antelope."

Coble blinked, glancing at String Bean. "Did that make any sense?"

"Not to me," String Bean said, moving stiffly, stretching his back. "But I'm just the deputy investigator."

The men moved toward the house, leaving the heavy draft horses swatting flies and chewing their bits. Coble walked ahead of them, steps deliberate, hand resting easy on his gun. The air smelled of dust and dry wood and something else he couldn't name, like turned earth, or rain that wouldn't come.

The house loomed larger as they neared, two stories high, the color faded where old white paint had peeled and weathered away. Shutters hung askew, and he made a note for repairs. A single curtain twitched in an upstairs window, too fast for wind.

Chapter Seven

Coble followed the tracks of a shod horse around to the back of the house. There was a small hitch rail fronting the back porch. He could see where the animal had stood for some time, probably tied and waiting. Judging from the tracks out front, whoever was inside saw them coming and left at a gallop. At least the horse did. The soft dirt next to the hitch rail showed small footprints going toward the house and none coming back. So, either a woman, a child, or a very small man. The width of the prints suggested a woman.

Holstering his belly gun, he climbed the steps and entered the house. Since he guessed a woman was inside, he assumed a lady in distress. Given his experience with women in his past, he should have known better.

Closing the back door, he turned and walked right into a woman holding a gun on him—a gun that was shaking even though held by two hands.

Startled, he spoke the first thing that came to his mind. "What happened to your horse?"

Startled, her voice quavered. "He ran away."

War Eagle and String Bean moved in from the front of the house, guns drawn. When they saw what was going on, they immediately holstered their revolvers.

"We did a quick run-through of the house, Boss. Looks like she's been living in one of the upstairs bedrooms."

Coble nodded. "Just her?"

"Looks like it, although there are some men's clothes in a valise."

She turned sharply toward War Eagle. "You leave those alone."

String Bean side-stepped to his left. When she tried to follow with the pistol, War Eagle stepped forward and gently took the gun from her hands.

"Ma'am," he said softly. "No harm will come to you here. You're safe."

When she slumped into a kitchen chair, Coble asked. "What's your name?"

The woman's voice was dull, shoulders slumped. She seemed as if all the fight was gone from her. "Adelina Morrow."

"So, call you Addy? Adelina is a mouthful." He guessed.

Her chin raised. "No. You may not."

String Bean quietly moved to the stove and began stoking a fire, then shook the coffeepot sitting on top. Grimacing, he started searching for coffee.

"Who belongs with the men's clothing?" Coble asked gently.

Showing a little life, she stared defiantly at Coble. "My father."

He nodded, encouraging her to speak. "Did he leave on that horse?"

"If he did, ghosts can ride."

"Ah." He glanced outside for a moment. "The extra grave. I'm sorry you lost your father. Was he hurt? Sick? Wounded?"

She shook her head. "No. Not really. He had a bad heart."

War Eagle watched her curiously. "How did you get here?"

"We had a wagon and two good draft horses. Those men must have followed me here and stolen them while I was inside taking care of my father."

"What men...exactly."

They listened with rapt attention to her story, keeping silent until she told of the three men they'd encountered.

"Did these men threaten you?" Coble asked.

"More like insinuated, but they weren't subtle." She shrugged. "If we hadn't held guns on them, I'm sure they'd have raped me, and my father and I killed. They were pretty plain about it."

"Well, now." He glanced at War Eagle. "Did you get a name by chance? Or would you recognize these men?"

"I'd know them anywhere. Things were a little tense." She stood abruptly. "I didn't think anyone lived here. I'm sorry to have trespassed. I...with my father's health, there wasn't much choice." Hands clutching a balled-up handkerchief, she continued in a small voice,

"Please don't hurt me. I'd leave, but I don't have any way to do that."

Coble shrugged. "Well, first thing. Like War Eagle said, you have nothing to fear from us. Period. And you were right. No one was living here when you arrived, so no fault there. The decision is all yours. We'll help if we can."

"Boss?" String Bean walked back into the kitchen, first adding coffee to the boiling water in the coffee pot. "Have you looked around? How long did you think this place had been vacant? Any idea?"

"Sure," Coble thought for a moment. "Three years, more or less."

"We've been upstairs and down. If there's a speck of dust anywhere, I can't find it. The floors are so shiny I'm afraid to walk on them. And the furniture is the same way. The only thing missing around here was coffee."

"I'm a compulsive cleaner, especially with such a fine home, and there was little else to do," the woman interjected. "And I ran out of coffee when they took my wagon."

Coble acknowledged the woman with a nod and then sighed, glancing at String Bean. "I suppose you have a point to make?"

"We're going to be ranching from daylight to dark, plus all the investigating you won't admit you want to do. Who's cleaning and taking care of this fine house? War Eagle?"

"Hey"—War Eagle backed up—"not me. I'll live in the barn first."

"As well you should," String Bean quipped, shaking his head.

"Excuse me?" Adeline interrupted in a soft voice, her gaze bouncing from each of their faces. "If you need someone, I can work and cook too."

"You don't even know us, ma'am," Coble said. "We could be terrible people."

"Not me," War Eagle said while taking off his hat and smoothing his hair. "I'm a saint."

String Bean started coughing, leaning against a kitchen counter.

"I know enough. If you were going to harm me, you'd have done it by now." She gave String Bean a concerned look. "I'm also desperately in need of a job. I've no money and no place to stay if I leave. There is precious little food here. Now, I don't even have a horse." She met the gaze of all three men. "I won't beg, but I will ask. May I be your housekeeper? Please?" Her face suddenly turned red. "That's not an invitation for anything else."

"No harm, remember?" Coble nodded. "Fine with me, at least for now. We'll see how it goes. Room and board, plus we'll pay you. Does that suit you?"

She smiled. "I accept."

"Good. If we bring in supplies, do you think you could rustle up some supper?"

"Of course. If you don't mind, just set whatever food supplies you have on the floor. I'll organize my own kitchen. And the first thing you can do is stomp the dirt off your boots before you come tracking in on my clean floor."

"Yes, ma'am," War Eagle said, giving his feet a guilty glance.

As they walked out the front, String Bean said, "I think someone's smitten."

"Smitten? Is that a word? What's that mean?" War Eagle said.

Coble laughed, feeling the most relaxed he'd been in a long time. "It means pay attention, or you'll fall off the porch."

THEY WORKED a couple of hours moving supplies inside to sit on the floor of the kitchen, once the table was full.

They'd purchased two rolls of barbed wire, and then found more rolls under scattered straw in one of the lean-to sheds. It was obvious no one had used the barn in a long time. Extra lumber was scattered throughout the barn, and they organized this against one wall. Coble didn't remember buying the lumber and wondered if the judge might have had some designs on the place. And why did he quit?

War Eagle kept casting glances toward the main house, seeming to find excuses to go to the large double doors.

They hobbled the horses on the grass behind the barn and then filled the water trough in the corral, carrying buckets from the well. The gate was left open so the stock could get to the water. Later, they'd put the horses up for the night. Coble didn't want to chance the thieves coming back for a second helping.

The trough at the windmill was filled to the brim. Standing on the platform under the windmill, Coble stared up at the squeaky apparatus.

Pushing the brake handle, he said, "Someone needs to climb up there and put some grease on those gears."

String Bean snorted. "Send War Eagle up there. He'd have a better view of the house."

Face turning beet red, War Eagle started marching toward his friend. "I've got a mind to—"

Coble stopped him with a hand on his chest. "You two knock it off. You don't need to be digging at each other all the time."

He turned and winked at String Bean. "Two bits says he shaves tonight."

A sudden loud clanging interrupted them. Turning toward the house, they saw Adelina running an iron rod around the triangle hanging from the eave of the porch. While still beating on the triangle, she yelled, "Supper is on."

Holding up his hand to stop the noise, Coble said, "We're right here, Adelina."

She gave them an embarrassed look. "I know. I've just always wanted to do that."

"Good. Glad you have that out of your system. We'll wash up and be in right away."

String Bean was already backing away when he yelled. "Does War Eagle have time to shave?"

His friends walked toward the house, bickering as usual. They seemed to be always at odds, but he pitied anyone who tried to get between them. He smiled at that. It had just been a few hours, but he figured if Adelina entertained War Eagle's advances, she'd have to find a woman for String Bean or take them both on. It wouldn't take much to foresee fireworks on the horizon.

His mind turned to the men who'd threatened Adelina and stolen her wagon and horses. And might have contributed to the death of her father, if he had a weak heart. Eyes narrowed in thought, he gazed toward the broken land between the ranch and Lamar. It wasn't just the law that was ingrained in him, though some would disagree. A strong sense of right and wrong still ruled his thoughts every day.

Warning bells had been ringing in his mind since the judge gave him back his ranch. It was a gamble, knowing nothing comes for free. He just had to figure out what was going on...who the players were...what the play was. Kind of like a poker game. Was there a card sharp in the mix? Or someone with a colossal bluff?

Coble watched quietly as the men gained the wash basins by the side door. In a short time, they'd breathed some life into the ranch, and there was a ton of work to do. In the distance, he could hear the creek passing over a riffle of gravel and limestone, whispering promises he felt more than heard.

He took a deep breath of the cooling evening air. Night birds fussed in the bushes while swallows swooped in the waning light. As he watched, a prairie falcon swept through like a bullet, and a fat pigeon exploded midair in a puffball of feathers.

It was a good thing he didn't believe in omens.

Chapter Eight

Lamar, Missouri, was a town bustling with wagon wheels and the scent of baking bread and fresh leather. The clang of a blacksmith's hammer carried down Main Street, mingling with the bray of mules and the steady hum of human endeavor. The prairie stretched endlessly to the west and north, broken only by split-rail fences and the slow, rippling tide of small cattle herds being driven to market in Kansas City. To the south, miners worked the stripped seams of coal and lead, their faces smudged and their laughter hard-edged. East of town, German farmers turned the black soil into neat furrows, coaxing corn and wheat from the stubborn ground.

It was 1881, and America was on the move—restless, hungry, and half-crazed with dreams. Wagon trains followed the railway north toward Kansas City, families bundled with all they owned, eyes fixed on a future they couldn't see but hoped might forgive them their pasts.

Lamar had become a crossing point, a nexus where new trails began and old ones ended. A locomotive pulling freight cars used the fresh spur line of the KATY, Missouri-Kansas-Texas railroad. Refueling twice a week with coal and water, delivering barrels, bolts of cloth, mining tools, gossip, and disease.

The confluence of humanity never stopped. Some came healthy and left broken, others arrived already half-dead. Bad food, dirty water, and worse luck. Lamar saw it all.

Mattie McKinney Hurst moved among them with the calm of a woman who had long since made peace with the fact that life and death slept in the same bed. At an age in her life where she was neither young nor old, her skirts rustled down the boardwalk, children tugging at the fabric with sticky hands, knowing she kept candy somewhere in her pockets.

Farmers lifted hats as she passed. Miners nodded or stopped her for a word of advice about a cough, a festering wound, a baby that wouldn't gain weight.

Her patients were mostly women and children, though she patched up men when they were shot, cut, or stepped on by their own horses. Men didn't like being doctored by a woman unless they were bleeding too badly to argue.

The town's last doctor had fled months ago. Rumor said it was over another man's wife and a badly timed escape through a second-story window. Her husband had given the man a choice between leaving and dying. Being an educated man and no fool, the doctor left. The wife's fate was less certain, the town pretended not to wonder.

So Mattie kept busy, and that was a blessing. Her

days began before dawn, and most nights she collapsed into dreamless sleep too deep for longing. It was better that way. Better not to lie awake missing a man who rode away years ago under a sky that had since forgotten his name.

Her daughters were far to the east, learning medicine at the same college she had attended, a school that had once refused to admit women until pressure—and persistence—made them yield. She was proud of them, proud and lonely. Now she was the only nurse, working as a physician, in a town that only half wanted her.

A huge black man stood by the clinic door, hat in hand, his shoulders broad enough to block out the sun. Amos had been her shadow for two years now, after she'd hired him from the Gentleman's Club next door, where he worked nights as a bouncer and peacemaker. He said he'd never been a slave, though the scars on his forearms and the careful watchfulness in his eyes hinted otherwise.

Mattie didn't pry. Amos was decent, strong, and carried a quiet wisdom that didn't comc from books.

More importantly, the town council had insisted she never treat a male patient without a male witness. *"For your protection,"* they'd said. Whether that protection was for her or her patients, she still wasn't sure. Just because the clinic was next to a saloon and whorehouse...

He nodded toward the door. "You got folks waiting, Miss Mattie."

"Do I?" She brushed her hands on her apron, already weary.

Amos leaned closer, voice low and warm, slow as

molasses. "There's a rumor going around that Coble Bray is back. Up near Runaway Creek. Setting up a ranch again."

The words stopped her mid-step. She knew exactly where the ranch was situated. Her breath hitched, an involuntary tremor threading through her composure. The name struck like a hammer on thin glass, sending memories scattering—sweat-soaked sheets, long silences by the fire, the smell of whiskey and gunpowder on his skin.

"Why would that matter to me?" She nearly stuttered, though both of them knew she was lying. Her daughters had written often, asking about Mr. Bray. And she knew that land well. She'd lived there once, when she'd still believed in new beginnings.

Before she could answer herself, the click of polished boots echoed behind her.

Deputy Joseph *Tibby* Thibodeaux, slicker than oiled parchment and twice as proud, stepped into the room carrying a spray of flowers and a smirk. His new suit caught the light, his hair gleamed from too much tonic.

"Miss Hurst," he drawled, "I thought your clinic might benefit from a bit of color this morning."

Mattie accepted the flowers with the grace of a woman accustomed to unwanted gifts. "Thank you, Deputy Thibodeaux. As you can see, I've got work to do."

He lingered, leaning one shoulder against the wall. His eyes roamed like a thief casing the place. "You're one of the few that can say my name right," he said. "Thibodeaux. Most folks tangle it up. It's endearing."

"Oh, I've met a Louisiana gambler or two," she said. "The accent tends to leave a mark."

He grinned. "But I'm no gambler."

"So you say," she said softly. "I expect you're something else entirely."

For a heartbeat, the air between them thickened. He took a step closer. Mattie's right hand drifted to the hidden pocket in her skirt, the one lined with leather that held her small revolver. The gesture was casual, unhurried, but deliberate.

"Was there something else, Deputy?"

He cleared his throat. "Only to extend an invitation. The new opera house is open. The players are said to be fine company."

Mattie sighed. "I'm sure they are, but I've patients to see and no taste for spectacle."

"Perhaps another night?" he pressed.

"Same answer, different day."

The deputy's smile didn't reach his eyes. "Then I'll leave you to your miracles, Miss Hurst. Enjoy the flowers."

He left a silence behind him that smelled faintly of pomade and menace.

Joanne, her assistant, watched the door close and snorted softly. "That man's too smooth by half."

Joanne worked at the saloon next door and knew men the way a gambler knew cards. Mousy hair, sharp tongue, and the kind of courage only found in women who've been hurt too many times.

"He's dangerous," she said simply.

Mattie nodded. "He is. And sometimes, smooth hides sharp edges." She gazed at the flowers for a long moment before setting them aside. "The trouble is, you never see the cut till it bleeds."

Before Joanne could reply, Amos's voice rumbled from the doorway. "Your first patient's ready. Man's got a furuncle on his backside. Says he wouldn't bother you with it, but he can't sit a saddle."

Mattie groaned. "Just what I need, a boil on a man's butt to start my morning. It's an omen, Amos."

He chuckled. "You asked why I mentioned Coble Bray," he said quietly.

Mattie froze mid-step again, the scalpel in her hand gleaming like a memory.

"Because," Amos went on, "you always ask about him when his name comes up. Always."

Her mind drifted back to that lonely ranch and two broken souls sharing grief and a bed. She'd been raw from burying her husband, and he'd been half-dead from losing his wife. What began as solace had turned into something that might have been love if the world had been kinder.

But the world never was.

"After what happened at that gambling town, Hard Times wasn't it?" Amos continued, "Folks thought he was done. But I have seen men like that. They don't stay gone. They circle back for what they want."

Mattie set the scalpel down and met his gaze. "Maybe. But he's a long shot, Amos. I'd sooner bet on the blackjack tables than Coble Bray walking through my door again."

Amos looked at her for a long moment, eyes deep and patient. "You're wrong about that. Coble will come. But so will Tibby. Both of them are headed your way, one for good and one for ill."

Mattie sighed, tightening the knot on her apron. "I'm not blind, Amos. I know sugar from salt. Now bring me the man with the boil before I start wishing I was back in St. Louis with decent patients."

He laughed softly as he opened the door.

But when she turned to wash her hands, she caught sight of her reflection in the small mirror above the basin. For just a flicker of a second, she thought she saw another face beside hers—a ghost of a man with hard eyes and a gentle voice, smiling like he still believed in second chances.

The sound of Amos's boots brought her back.

"All right," she said briskly, setting her jaw. "Let's see if we can save this man's dignity...and my morning."

Outside, a freight train's whistle wailed across the prairie, long and low, like a promise carried on the wind. She often wondered if it brought trouble or took it away.

THE MAN with the boil turned out to be a ranch hand from the north end of Jasper County, young enough to still blush when Mattie told him to drop his trousers and bend over the table. His name was Clyde, and he'd ridden twenty miles in the saddle before admitting he could hardly sit in it.

"Lord above," she muttered, swabbing the inflamed skin. "You wait until it gets this bad, then come calling. Men will die before they admit they're in pain."

Clyde winced. "Didn't figure it was proper to have a lady doctor look at my...uh—"

"But a lady can give birth to you, feed you, and

wash your butt until you're big enough to do it on your own?" Mattie gave him a cool glance. "I assure you, young man, I've seen worse, and on better men. Now hold still."

Amos, standing just inside the door, folded his arms and looked everywhere but at the patient. The big man's presence was enough to keep any notions of impropriety in check, though Clyde's face turned as red as a beet.

When she made the incision, the young man yelped loud enough to startle sparrows perched by the window. Mattie worked efficiently, her hands steady. Years of stitching wounds and birthing babies had turned her into a machine of calm purpose when facing blood or pain.

When it was done, she bandaged him neatly and gave him a small jar of ointment. "Twice a day, and stay off that horse for two days. When you run out of that, use honey. It does well with infection."

Clyde fidgeted. "Can't, ma'am. Got to drive cattle to market. The herd's passing by as we speak."

"Then you'll have a bigger problem next time," she said firmly. "You'll end up septic, and no amount of prayer will save you. Tell your boss Dr. Hurst said so."

Her tone left no room for argument. Clyde thanked her awkwardly and shuffled out, walking like a man with a secret he wished he'd kept.

"Dr. Hurst?"

"Hell, they don't know the difference."

Amos chuckled. "You surely enjoy scaring those boys half to death."

She wiped her hands clean. "Better fear than ignorance." Then, quieter, she said, "And it keeps them alive."

Outside, a wagon rumbled past, and Mattie paused by the open door. Dust hung in the air, glowing gold in the morning light. The streets of Lamar bustled with life—horses clopping, voices raised in barter, the faint strains of a fiddle from the saloon.

But beneath it all, something restless stirred in her bones. The news of Coble Bray wouldn't leave her mind. She could almost see him leaning against a post, hat brim low, with those storm-gray eyes that missed nothing.

Coble Bray. The name alone was trouble wrapped in leather and gunpowder.

He'd left her without promises, just a kiss and a half-smile that said he wanted to come back but didn't trust himself to do it. Men like him didn't belong to anyone, they belonged to the road, to vengeance, to whatever ghost of a cause still drove them forward.

Still...she'd never stopped listening for hoofbeats in the night, or his whisper-quiet tread coming to her door.

Joanne appeared at her elbow, holding a tray of medicine bottles. "You're thinking again," she said. "I can always tell. Your face goes all soft, like you're seeing something no one else can."

Mattie smiled faintly. "Maybe I am."

"You're thinking of that Coble feller, ain't you?"

Mattie stiffened. "You've been listening to Amos too much."

Joanne shrugged. "Hard not to. He's right about a lot of things." She set down the tray, eyes bright with mischief and warning alike. "You know, the deputy was sniffing around the Gentleman's Club again. Asked about you."

Mattie turned sharply. "What did he want?"

"Said he was curious if you kept late hours. Asked if you ever took to drinking."

Mattie's expression hardened. "That's none of his business."

Joanne nodded. "Exactly what Amos said. He told the deputy you didn't need watching, that you needed respect. Tibby didn't take kindly to that."

"Let him stew," Mattie muttered. But she felt a chill run down her spine. Tibby Thibodeaux was the sort of man who didn't like being denied, especially by a woman.

By late afternoon, the clinic quieted. Mattie stepped outside to breathe, the sunlight slanting across the street in long amber bars. She stood by the hitching post, arms folded, watching a freight wagon loaded with barrels marked *KEROSENE—HANDLE WITH CARE*. The driver's boy struggled with the harness, and Mattie went to help, her fingers deftly fixing the buckle.

"Thank you, ma'am," the boy said shyly.

"You're welcome," she replied. "Tell your pa to keep an eye on that rear wheel. She's loose on the pin."

She watched them trundle away, then turned toward the horizon. Beyond the rooftops, the prairie shimmered like an ocean of gold. Somewhere out there, maybe near Runaway Creek, was a man she'd once loved.

She almost smiled. "Fools," she whispered. "Both of us."

Amos's voice came from behind her. "You talking to yourself again?"

"Maybe," she said softly. "I'm a good listener."

He nodded toward the street. "Then you'd best get your mind sharp. Look who's coming."

Mattie followed his gaze and saw Deputy Thibodeaux again, swaggering across the road like he owned it. His hat was tilted just so, his silver badge gleaming in the late sun.

She groaned. "Not again."

"Seems like he forgot something," Amos murmured.

Tibby tipped his hat as he approached. "Evening, Miss Hurst. Thought I might walk you home once you close up."

Mattie's jaw tightened. "No need. I'm sure you know I live in this building. It's not like I need an escort to pass through a door."

"I'm sure you don't," Tibby said smoothly. "Still, a lady alone...it's a rough town after dark. I could ensure your safety...wherever you are."

Amos stepped forward slightly, a quiet wall of muscle. "She ain't alone, Mr. Tibby."

For a moment, Tibby's charm cracked, his eyes narrowing. "I was speaking politely, Amos. No cause to puff up."

"Then best keep it polite," Amos said evenly. "Miss Mattie don't need company she didn't ask for."

A long silence stretched between the two men, as taut as a tripwire. The deputy's fingers brushed his belt near the butt of his revolver, and Mattie's hand itched toward her hidden pocket.

Trying to defuse the situation, she commented. "Thank you for your concern, Deputy."

Tibby's smile was thin and false, more dangerous because of his capitulation. "Didn't mean any disrespect. Y'all have a fine evening."

He tipped his hat again and strolled off toward the saloon, whistling a tune that sounded just a little too careless.

Mattie exhaled slowly. "That man's a snake," she said.

Amos grunted. "And snakes don't bite until you stop watching."

The sun was setting now, the sky bruised purple and gold. Mattie locked the clinic door and walked to the living quarters in the back of the building. Amos had bid her good night and walked next door to the saloon, his night job. The streetlamps flickered to life one by one as she glanced out the window, kerosene flames guttering in the wind. The man on stilts drifted by, aloof from the barking dogs and children puttering around below. Maybe that's what she needed...stilts to keep above the fray.

She paused, listening. The night carried familiar sounds—crickets, distant laughter from the saloon, a piano playing "Camptown Races." But beneath it all was something else. A whisper. The faint echo of hooves on the hard-packed road leading in from the north.

She turned her head, squinting into the dark.

Nothing moved, yet her heart pounded. It was

probably nothing, but sometimes nothing is just something waiting to happen.

Mattie looked out toward the road that led to Runaway Creek. She could almost see a lone rider cresting the hill, his hat low, his face shadowed. Coble Bray had a way of arriving when she least expected him.

She thought of the deputy's wintry smile, of Amos's warning, of the quiet dread that came before storms.

Chapter Nine

It had been a frustrating week. Runaway Creek was proving to be an enigma—beautiful, dangerous, and wholly unpredictable. From the front porch of the ranch house, it looked innocent enough, winding lazily past the corrals and shimmering like polished glass under the morning sun. It gave easy access to water for the horses, kept the grass green through dry months, and even offered a clean pool or two for a man to wash the dust off after a long day.

But farther south, where the hills began to roll like sleeping giants, the creek showed its teeth. Floods over the years had carved a deep gash into the land, a gorge hundreds of feet wide with limestone walls slick as soap. Scrubby cedar and willow clung to the edges, their roots twisting like fingers desperate for a grip. Down below, the creek coiled through pools of clear water, whispering to itself as if it remembered a time when it had run straight and gentle.

Coble sat on his horse near the edge, the animal shifting uneasily beneath him. He studied the problem, thumb rubbing the worn leather of his reins, while War Eagle and String Bean loaded posts and wire into the wagon. Sweat darkened their shirts, and the smell of hot iron and horses hung in the still air.

"Well, this has been fun," War Eagle groused, shoving his gloves into his back pocket. "This gorge is a natural trap for cattle, and there ain't much we can do about it."

They'd spent most of the day fighting the ground. The limestone was too shallow for posts, and every hole they tried to dig turned up more rock than dirt.

"How far back from the edge before we get dirt deep enough for a post?" Coble asked.

"Too far," String Bean sighed, collapsing into the wagon seat with a creak of wood and leather. "Fifteen, twenty feet at least. We could build a fence there, but once a critter gets between it and the gorge, they're penned in like a fool."

"Horses will figure it out," War Eagle said. "Dumb cow critters will just fall in."

Coble let his gaze drift along the jagged cut of land. "Wonder how this happened. The creek looks tame everywhere else."

"Could be mining upstream," String Bean said. "I heard there was a claim or two up past the ridge a few years back. If they loosened the soil, the floods might have chewed straight through to bedrock."

Coble nodded. "Makes sense. You see the high-water marks on those trees? Some of that debris is fifteen feet up. That's a hell of a flood."

"Which means it'll bring the water right up to the barn next time," Coble added, mopping sweat with his handkerchief. "Maybe we'd do better shoring up the outbuildings before the next storm takes 'em."

String Bean squinted up at the brassy sky. Heat shimmered like smoke above the prairie grass. "You think it's gonna rain that much again? Ever?"

"If it's done it once, it'll do it again," Coble said. "That's the way of things."

The three men sat quiet for a while. The only sounds were the faint hiss of cicadas and the occasional rattle of the wagon as the wind passed through the wire rolls.

"So what about the gorge?" String Bean asked finally.

Coble exhaled. "We leave it. We can't win a fight against limestone and floodwater. Maybe we just need to breed smarter cattle."

That got a laugh out of War Eagle. "Speaking of which," he said, "we need to get a herd going. Pasture's going to waste out there."

"I've been thinking about that," Coble said.

War Eagle grinned. "Thought I smelled something burning."

Coble ignored him. "We're not set up for a big herd. Not yet. I don't plan to hire a bunch of hands, and I don't see us turning this place into one of those outfits that run a thousand head and lose half of 'em to weather. In a few years, this'll be farmland. A good part already is."

He turned in the saddle to look toward the north fields, where the land flattened and green prairie shimmered faintly under the sun. "I'd rather run a few horses, keep enough cattle for our own needs, and build around the barns. Corrals, pens—something that'll last."

"To what end?" String Bean asked.

"To keep us living steady," Coble said. "Gardens fenced against rabbits and wind. A few goats for milk, chickens for eggs, maybe a couple hogs for bacon and ham. That sort of thing."

War Eagle wrinkled his nose. "I ain't built to be a sodbuster."

"You're not built to be a cattle baron either," Coble said with a half-smile. "Let's call ourselves gentleman farmers. Between the three of us, we can make it work."

String Bean leaned forward, elbows on knees. "Which leaves time for...?"

Coble's eyes narrowed. "Maybe nosing around a little. We've still got the judge's brother to think about."

War Eagle snorted. "Or maybe time to convince that new cook of ours I'm a god among men."

String Bean grinned. "That'll take a miracle, not time. They do say that if you tell a lie often enough, it can become fact."

"Hey," War Eagle shot back, mock-wounded, "all she's gotta do is look at me."

Coble chuckled. "Alright, gentlemen. War Eagle and I will work around the barns, reinforcing where we can. String Bean, you've got the best sense for stock. Check around the neighboring farms, see what's for sale. There might be an auction in Lamar—look into it."

"I'll do it," String Bean said, picking up the reins.

Coble tipped his hat against the glare. "Good. Let's

haul this gear back before the heat cooks us. Feels like the kind of day that ends in thunder."

The three of them turned the wagon toward the ranch. The horses trudged slowly through the tall grass. Behind them, Runaway Creek glimmered in the sun—bright, calm, and secretive—like something waiting for its moment to rise again.

THE WAGON WHEELS creaked in rhythm with the plod of hooves. Dust lifted from the dry grass and drifted behind them in lazy clouds. The land stretched wide and gold beneath a hard sun, the air so still it felt like even the flies were too tired to find them.

By the time they reached the barn, the sky had changed. What had been brassy and blinding now dulled into a washed-out yellow-gray. To the southwest, thunderheads were climbing the horizon—tall, dark towers and bruised purple underneath, connected by chain lightning.

"Guess you were right," String Bean said. "Looks like your floodwater's coming sooner than later."

"Eh, it's hard to tell." Coble swung down from his horse and looped the reins over a fence post. "Could just be heat lightning. But we'd better not bet the stock on it."

War Eagle wiped sweat and dust from his face with his hat brim. "I'll get the mares inside. We don't want them spooked by thunder."

The smell of rain rode faint on the wind now, clean and sharp, carrying the promise of relief from the heat

—or ruin for the unprepared. In a land begging for moisture, you take the bad with the good.

———

INSIDE THE BARN, it was dim and stuffy. Dust motes floated in the narrow beams of light cutting through gaps in the siding. The men worked with little talk, each with his own rhythm: War Eagle checking harnesses and stall doors, String Bean forking newly purchased hay, Coble stacking the remaining posts against the wall.

After a while, the sound of hammering thunder faded, replaced by the gentle rattle of wind against the boards.

"Y'know," String Bean said after a moment, "when I was a boy, my pa used to say a quiet day before a storm is God's way of letting you think about what you've done."

War Eagle snorted. "You must've spent a lot of time thinking, then."

String Bean grinned. "Is that why you never do it? Too scared of what might come up?"

Their laughter echoed in the rafters, low and easy, the kind that comes only from men who've seen each other at their best and worst.

Coble smiled faintly, leaning against a stall gate. For a moment, he let himself imagine the ranch as it could be—a place of order and calm, fenced fields, horses grazing under a steady sun, the creek quiet for good. But even as the thought formed, thunder cracked in the distance, reminding him how little peace ever lasted.

"Storm's moving fast," War Eagle said, peering through the barn door. "Sky's turning green out there. It's going to be dumping a ton of water upstream."

String Bean nodded. "I'd rather it rained hard here. That way, all the runoff would go away from us."

"Get the shutters closed on the house," Coble said. "And make sure the chickens are in the coop this time, not hiding under the porch to be coyote food."

War Eagle rolled his eyes but went.

The first drops fell, a heavy, uneven patter on the tin roof. Then came the wind, whistling down the valley and carrying the scent of wet earth.

By the time they reached the house, the cook, Adelina, was standing on the porch, apron whipping in the wind. "Took you long enough," she called over the rising noise. "I told you this storm would hit before supper."

War Eagle grinned, stepping past her. "You just missed me too much, that's all."

She swatted at him with a towel. "Miss the smell of sweat and horsehair? I don't think so."

Coble ducked inside, hiding a smile. It was pretty clear that War Eagle had already won that battle.

The house felt solid, built from hand-cut timber and care. The smell of stew hung heavy in the air, thick with onions and something savory.

"Dinner will be ready in an hour," Adelina said, slamming the door against the wind.

Coble hung his hat on the peg by the door and looked out the window. The rain was coming hard now —sheets of water slanting sideways, hammering the earth flat. Lightning flickered white across the fields, showing the line of the creek far off, already rising.

He watched a moment longer, uneasy. Runaway Creek was living up to its name again.

"Tomorrow," he breathed, almost to himself. "We'll see what's left."

String Bean turned from the table, where he had been playing with spoons, waiting expectantly for supper. "You think it'll get that bad?"

Coble didn't answer. He just watched the lightning flash again, the reflection glinting in his eyes. Outside, thunder rolled through the hills like the deep growl of something ancient waking up.

And for a fleeting second, he could've sworn he heard the creek roaring back—alive, angry, and closer than it had any right to be.

"I'd say tomorrow will be interesting."

THE STORM BROKE HARD through the night.

Wind howled across the hills like something wild and grieving, shaking the windows in their frames, even though the shutters were closed. Rain hammered the roof in waves, sometimes steady, sometimes in furious bursts that made the eaves shudder. More than once, lightning struck close enough to light the entire house like noonday. Each flash revealed shadows frozen mid-motion—the boots by the hearth, the iron stove, Adelina's worried face as she checked for leaks along the upstairs ceiling.

By dawn, the wind had died. The world lay hushed and exhausted.

Coble was the first outside at daylight. The air smelled of wet cedar and earth, and the mist hung thick over the fields. His boots sank deep into the mud with every step. The storm had stripped leaves from the trees, scattered branches across the yard, and left the chicken coop half-collapsed against the fence. Maybe he should have put them under the porch.

But the house still stood. The barn, too.

He looked toward the creek.

At first glance, it seemed unchanged—still and silver beneath the morning light—but when he climbed the small rise beyond the corral, he saw what the night had done. Runaway Creek had swelled past its banks, sweeping away everything that had dared to come too close. Fences lay broken. A wagon wheel, half-buried in silt, jutted from the mud. One of the limestone walls upstream had crumbled, leaving a fresh scar where the gorge had widened another twenty feet.

Coble pulled his hat low and swore under his breath.

War Eagle joined him a few minutes later, eyes red from lack of sleep. "Whole north fence is down," he said. "Lucky the stock stayed put. Guess they were smarter than we gave 'em credit for."

"Or too tired to care," Coble muttered.

String Bean came slogging up the hill behind them, his pants plastered with mud. "I walked down toward the lower pasture," he said. "Creek jumped its bed again. There's a washout near the ford—a big one. You could lose a wagon in it."

Coble's stomach sank. "Any sign of the cattle in that section?"

"Tracks heading uphill. They'll be fine," String

Bean said. "But you'll want to see this." He motioned for them to follow.

After saddling their horses, they rode out slowly, the animals uneasy in the muck, hooves sloshing through puddles that mirrored the pale sky. The land felt different—tilted somehow, rearranged by the storm's temper.

When they reached the washed-out ford, Coble dismounted. What had been a shallow crossing was now a twenty-foot drop into swirling brown water. The limestone shelf beneath had given way completely, leaving a fresh overhang that creaked and groaned as the current tore at its edges.

And there, caught between two jutting stones, was something that didn't belong.

Coble crouched low. It was a wooden beam, squared and fitted, half-covered in silt and tangled weeds. He brushed it clean with his glove. Carved into the surface, faint but unmistakable, was a mark—a letter S enclosed in a circle.

He looked up sharply. "You recognize this?"

String Bean squinted. "Looks like a branding mark."

"It is," Coble said quietly. "Judge Stone's brand."

War Eagle frowned. "That's nearly thirty miles upstream."

"More like thirty-five," Coble said, eyes narrowing. "And his brother disappeared around there."

"He's a marshal, isn't he?" String Bean shrugged when no answer came.

The three men stood silent, listening to the creek's restless murmur.

Finally, String Bean spoke again. "You think that storm washed something down?"

"I think," Coble said slowly, "it might have uncovered something that wasn't meant to be found."

Thunder rumbled far off to the south—leftover growl from the night before. Coble straightened, the wet wind tugging at his coat. The land smelled raw, unsettled, and alive.

"Let's get a rope around this and tie it off to a tree," he said. "It's too late to do this tonight. Hopefully, we can get this out before the creek takes it again."

War Eagle grinned grimly. "And if it's what I think it is?"

Coble swung into the saddle. "Then Runaway Creek's not the only thing with secrets."

Chapter Ten

THE SOUND OF THE CREEK FILLED THE MORNING with a steady, low rumble, like an old beast breathing under the earth. Mist drifted off the water, wrapping the gorge in thin veils of silver that broke and reformed with every gust. The sun was still low, a pale coin in the east, its light too thin to warm the stones.

Coble, War Eagle, and String Bean came down the slope slowly, leading their horses by the reins. Ropes, shovels, and a pry bar hung from the saddles, clanking with each step. The animals wanted no part of it. They snorted and tossed their heads, hooves sliding on wet clay, the whites of their eyes showing. The air carried something sour, not the usual rot of the riverbank, but older, heavier, the smell of something that should've stayed buried.

The timber beam jutted from the mud like a bone through flesh. It had been half-hidden when they found it yesterday, but the storm overnight had scoured more of the bank clean. Now, with the morning mist clinging low, it looked like the earth had coughed up part of its own skeleton. The carved S at its end caught what little light there was, faint but unmistakable.

War Eagle crouched first, pressing his palm to the grain, feeling its damp cold. "You sure it's the same mark?" he asked.

Coble nodded. "Judge Stone branded everything that came out of his mill. Logs, crates, wagon planks... even coffins. That's his work."

"Bridge timber, maybe?" String Bean offered, but there was no conviction in his voice.

"Bridge wasn't built this solid," War Eagle said, still crouched, running his fingers along the seams. "See that joint on the corner? Cross-braced. Box frame. Something sealed up."

Coble took the end of the shovel and scraped more silt away, careful and slow. The blackened wood was still strong. "It shouldn't be here," he said quietly. "The Stone Mill is twenty miles south."

"High water," War Eagle commented, "can take one county to the next."

They dug in silence after that, falling into the rhythm of labor, scrape, heave, and breathe. The wet clay sucked at their boots. Each shovel of earth released the sharp stink of river mud, sour as old blood. It clung to their sleeves and gloves. The work was hard, but the silence was harder. Even the birds had gone still.

After half an hour, the outline took shape to be six feet long, maybe two wide, with squared corners, nailed tight. Coble stepped back, his breath misting in the chill air.

"That's no bridge timber," he said.

String Bean swallowed. "Looks more like a crate."

War Eagle's gaze met Coble's. "It's a coffin."

No one disagreed. The word hung between them, heavy as lead.

The wind shifted then, coming up the gorge, carrying a faint odor of decay sealed too long.

Coble crouched again, scraping mud from the edges. The carved S looked older now, its lines softened by water and abrasion. He ran his thumb along the groove, feeling the faint tremor in his own hand.

"Help me with this," he said quietly.

They looped ropes around the corners, braced their boots, and pulled. The suction fought them every inch. The mud clung to the box like a hand that didn't want to let go. Finally, with a wet, sucking groan, it broke free. Water filled the hollow where it had lain, dark and cold.

Coble stood over it, mud up to his knees. "Let's get it open."

"Uh...why?" String Bean asked.

"We need to get an idea of where this came from so we can return it."

They wedged the pry bar under the edge, working slow, each crack of splitting wood echoing down the gorge. The lid came loose with a wet pop, a rank breath of trapped air escaping, a foul rush that made all three men flinch.

Inside lay a tangle of burlap and canvas, stiff and dark with age. For a moment, none of them moved. Then War Eagle reached in, his face set, and pulled back the fabric.

A skull stared up at them, yellowed bone grinning through scraps of black, leathered flesh. The sockets were hollow, and a few teeth still clung to the jaw. The rags of a shirt clung to the shoulders, faded to ghost-gray.

No one spoke.

Coble crouched, voice low. "Easy, now. The dead can't hurt you."

He brushed away a handful of silt near the ribs. Something caught the light. A length of tarnished chain. He pulled it free, and at the end, a silver badge dulled by years in the dark.

He turned it in his palm, rubbing the grime away with his thumb. The engraving was faint but legible in the pale light.

Deputy US Marshal Eli Stone.

String Bean stepped back, making a small sign across his chest. "The judge's brother," he said hoarsely.

War Eagle stood silent, his eyes fixed on the box. "Guess we found him."

Coble closed the lid gently, the wood creaking as it settled, nails seated in their groove. The mist had thinned by now, and sunlight lanced through the canyon in thin beams. The creek ran on beside them, steady, uncaring.

"No," Coble said finally. "We found what's left of him." He looked out across the gorge. "I guess this is one mystery that's solved."

For a while, there was no sound but the water and the crows circling high above. One called, sharp and lonely, before drifting north toward the ridge.

War Eagle broke the silence. "Seems to me the judge asked you to find his brother. You've done that. It's a rarity that someone dies of ill intent and then gets put in a casket built from wood from his brother's mill. I'd say natural causes, and nobody sought to inform the judge."

Coble didn't answer right away. He stood with the badge in his hand, turning it over, reading the years worn into it. "Pack it up," he said finally. "We'll take the badge to town and dump this mess on the sheriff's lap. He has jurisdiction over this, so he can do the notifying. We'll bury the casket out back behind the house. After that, it's not our problem. But not a word to anyone else, not until we know what we're walking into."

War Eagle gave a low whistle. "Runaway Creek sure has some secrets."

Coble nodded, eyes on the flowing water. "Maybe. But it just gave one back."

THE WORK of pulling the box clear was slow and ugly. They lashed the ropes around it, heaved in rhythm, sliding it across wet clay toward the slope. Every few feet, it stuck again, sucking at the ground like the earth didn't want to part with it. By the time they reached the horses, all three men were slick with sweat and mud.

String Bean wiped his face with his sleeve. "Feels wrong, digging him up just to put him back down."

"He wasn't down, he was traveling on floodwater." War Eagle checked the knots on the lashings. "Feels wrong leaving him in the mud like a dead fish."

Coble tightened the cinch strap, tying the coffin to a travois they'd fashioned from fence rails. "He wore the badge. That's enough to earn him dirt under the sky."

They started up the incline, the horses straining, nostrils flared. The travois creaked behind them, dragging through gravel and roots. Above, the light was clearer, the wind sharper. The mist clung below them like a sea, and the gorge disappeared into white.

At the ridge, they rested the animals. From here, they could see the valley opening wide, the thin line of Runaway Creek cutting through cottonwoods, the faint rise of Lamar to the east. Beyond that, nothing but prairie rolling to the edge of the world.

Coble squatted by the travois, staring at the black box. His reflection shimmered faintly in the water pooled atop the lid. "Judge said his brother went missing two years ago," he said. "Headed south on a warrant and never came back."

War Eagle spat into the dirt. "Guess he found what he was looking for."

"Or someone made sure he didn't."

String Bean shifted uneasily. "You think Tibby knew about this?"

Coble looked up sharply. "Why bring him into it?"

"I don't know," String Bean said. "Just seems... everything's circling the same whirlpool lately. Like that eddy out there in the creek that just pulls everything toward it."

They rode the rest of the way in silence.

BY THE TIME they reached the ranch, the sun was high, and the day had grown heavy. Biting flies buzzed lazily around the horses' flanks. Adelina was waiting on the porch, one hand shading her eyes, the other resting on the shotgun propped against the post.

"What's that you've got tied up?" she called as they approached.

"Trouble," String Bean muttered.

Coble dismounted, dust and mud falling from him in clumps. "Found something down by the creek."

Her gaze dropped to the box. "That a body?"

Coble nodded. "Used to be."

Adelina came down the steps, skirts brushing the dirt. "You're bringing ghosts home now?"

"Not by choice."

She studied his face, saw the set of his jaw, and said nothing more. Instead, she fetched a spade and followed them around to the back of the house, where a mother and a father lay.

The earth was dry near the surface, but turned dark and cool deeper down. The sound of shovels hitting rock carried across the yard. When it was done, they lowered the box in with ropes, the wood thudding softly against the bottom.

Coble stood at the edge, hat in hand. The badge glinted once in the sunlight before he returned it to his pocket. "Deputy Marshal Eli Stone," he said quietly. "Found in the mud, laid to rest in the dirt. Better company now than he had before."

War Eagle bowed his head. String Bean shuffled his feet awkwardly, murmuring something half-prayer, half-curse. Adelina watched them all with unreadable eyes.

When the grave was filled, Coble smoothed the

mound with the back of the spade. "We tell no one until I talk to the sheriff."

Adelina nodded slowly. "You think he didn't already know?"

Coble looked up sharply. "What are you saying?"

"Judges keep their secrets tighter than creek mud," she said. "You think he didn't wonder where his brother went? You think he didn't send anyone before you?"

Coble didn't answer. His jaw worked, and his eyes went to the horizon where the ridges met the sky.

"You don't sound too trusting. Have you met Judge Stone?"

"Don't have to...he's a judge."

String Bean cleared his throat. "What about the sheriff?"

"It's his jurisdiction, but I doubt he'll be interested."

War Eagle leaned on his shovel. "What if he takes an interest in it?"

Coble's eyes were hard now. "I guess we'll cross that bridge when we come to it."

"Well, you might take notice," War Eagle said. "Most of our bridges are floating away."

THAT EVENING, as dusk fell, Coble sat on the porch with his coffee, watching the light fade from the hills. The air smelled of wet earth and hickory smoke. The horses grazed near the fence, their shapes fading into shadow.

War Eagle came out and dropped into the chair

beside him, wood creaking under his weight. "You still turning it over?"

Coble nodded. "That deputy didn't just accidentally get buried. Family...somebody had to do that."

"You think the judge had a hand in it?"

"His own brother? I don't know," Coble said. "If he did, why ask us to find out why he disappeared? But I know this, his mill used those same crates. And I know Eli Stone was found in one of them. Usually, cemeteries aren't situated close to waterways for several reasons. The same reason you don't have a barn lot uphill from your well. Which leads me to believe the judge's brother was planted by himself close to the creek, where eventually, flood waters washed him out. All guesswork, of course. But it's enough to start asking questions."

War Eagle took a sip of coffee. "Careful asking them. Folks with power don't like ghosts showing up at breakfast."

"Neither do I," Coble said softly.

Out by the creek, frogs had started their night chorus. The air turned cool, and a soft wind stirred the squeaking blades of the windmill.

Adelina stepped onto the porch, lighting a lantern. Its glow caught in her hair, warm against the encroaching dark. "You planning on sleeping at all, Coble?"

Coble shook his head. "Not yet."

She casually leaned a hip against War Eagle's shoulder. "Y'all need your rest."

The wind carried the sound of the low rushing creek from the gorge, the same steady voice that had whispered through the morning mist. It sounded like it was speaking to itself, telling stories of what it had taken and what it had finally chosen to give back.

Coble stared into the distance, where the horizon burned faintly red beneath the coming night.

"Runaway Creek keeps its secrets," War Eagle said again, almost to himself.

"Maybe," Coble murmured. "But it doesn't keep 'em forever."

The three of them sat there in silence as the light drained away, the sound of the creek folding into the dark—quiet, patient, eternal.

Chapter Eleven

THE STORM HAD PASSED BY MORNING, LEAVING THE world clean-smelling of pine and cedar, washing the dust away, revealing the bright colors of gaily painted window frames and doors. Mist still clung to the low hills, curling around the trees like smoke.

Coble maneuvered his horse past small rivers of water running down the street, watching men trying to move wagons sunk to the hubs in mud, while horses struggled hock-deep in the quagmire. Prairie soil is hard as a rock when dry. When wet, there's no bottom to it. He rode slowly around the fringes, keeping to the dryer edges, in no hurry to injure his horse in the circus called Main Street after a heavy rain.

Still, he took a deep, lung-filling breath, reveling in the coolness after the summer heat. Grinning at people yelling and screaming at mired wagons in helpless situations, it was still a good day. The only winner in this situation was a man with a team of mules, lots of rope, and a penchant for free enterprise.

A woman hanging clothing on a line stretched

between two trees gave him directions, and they were sound. At the north end of town, next to a large, two-story building labeled Lamar Gentleman's Club, a smaller building sported a sign painted in block letters, Medical Clinic. The building's white paint faded to gray, chipped and peeling, weary of fighting the prairie winds.

His first thought was that most of her business might come from the saloon next door, but the housewife he'd questioned had nothing but glowing praise for Mattie Hurst.

He'd thought long and hard about bringing this problem to her doorstep, knowing he was more the problem than a skull fished from the creek. They'd parted on good terms, sort of. But as time stretched out, jobs came one after the other until everything got away from him. Now, his guilt made him reluctant to face her.

Mattie was a crack shot, he'd seen it. Serving a brief time as a trick-shot artist in a carnival, she was the best snap-shooter he'd ever seen, himself included. He figured it was fifty-fifty that she wouldn't shoot him on sight.

Tying his horse to the hitch rail, he untied the gunny sack from the pommel of the saddle and stepped onto the porch. Before he could move to the door, a huge black man seemed to materialize from nowhere. Coble tried to sidestep and go inside, but the man stepped in front of him.

"Do you have business here?" The man's voice was low, with no hint of animosity. A small smile graced the man's face as he gazed at Coble.

Coble stood for a moment, staring at the man.

He'd seen some big men, his mind flashing back to Tomlin Harp, or The Pianoman, who bent iron bars to escape jail. This man looked just as formidable.

"So, are you a doorman, someone to screen patients...what?" Coble asked.

The affable giant nodded. "My name's Amos, and you got it in one guess. The town council felt it to be safer for all gentlemen patients to be accompanied inside. Some people don't treat female doctors with respect, and the council felt this would be more proper."

Contemplating that for a moment, Coble nodded and smiled. The man was correct. "Seems like a wise precaution. And I'm sure that also goes for giant doormen of color. Look, I have business with Mattie, and she knows me. Anything else is none of your concern." Coble took a step back, blurting as the man squared up in front of him, "If you don't mind."

Amos asked in a rumbling voice. "May I say who's calling?"

"Coble Bray."

The big man's demeanor changed as a smile washed over his face. "Ah. You're the one exception to the rule, Mr. Bray."

He gestured for Coble to step by. "Have a good day, sir."

Coble glanced at the door. "Actually, I'd appreciate it if you'd stand in front of me when I go inside. It's even money whether I get a kiss or a lead ball."

Amos laughed and shook his head. When the man stepped away, Coble swore it changed the airflow along the porch. Shaking his head, he moved through the door.

Inside, the place smelled of carbolic and lavender oil. Open windows moved an array of curtains with a soft breeze. A small fire crackled in the stove, heating a pan of water placed on the flat top, and Mattie—hair tied back, sleeves rolled to her elbows—was washing instruments in soapy, steaming water.

"I'll be with you in a moment." When he didn't comment, she looked up, startled. "Coble Bray," she whispered. "I prayed you'd find your way back here someday."

He took off his hat and laid the sack by the door.

"What are you doing here?" Her voice was barely audible.

He shrugged. "Had some questions and thought you'd have the best answers. Besides, I wanted to check on you."

"I've been waiting for three years for you to check on me," she breathed. "And it was your second choice? I was about to give up."

Hat in hand, he stood awkwardly, shifting his weight from one foot to the other. "You said you wouldn't wait for me...and I didn't blame you. Figured you to be married by now."

"I lied." She gave him a long, intense look and then moved up to him, brushing his hat to the side and then tossing it on the floor. She surprised him with a long, thorough kiss, molding her body to his, soaking his shirt with her soapy arms.

Finally released, he said, "You stopped smoking."

Not answering, she slid around him and opened the door. "Amos? I'll be closed for the rest of the day... unless someone is blown up or shot."

"Yes, ma'am." The reply was more chuckle than speech. "I'll see to it."

Turning, she grabbed Coble by the shirtfront, pulling him toward the back of the building.

"Mattie, I—"

"Shut up, Coble. It's been three years, and I have an itch. I can always shoot you later."

EVENING FOUND them finishing a beef stew, sitting at a small table in the back apartment. Larger than it appeared from the street, the front two rooms served as a waiting room and treatment area. The back of the building had several rooms.

Surprised by the layout, Coble said, "Seems like a nice place you have here."

She snorted. "Big area out front? Lots of smaller rooms in the back? Next door to a gentleman's club? Betcha can't guess what it used to be."

Smiling, he looked at the place in a new light. "So why not now? What happened?"

"They built an upstairs next door. More efficient. So," she continued, pinning him with a steady gaze, "the big question. Why now? Why didn't you come home? The girls missed you. I missed you."

"Wish I could give you a good reason." He shifted uncomfortably in his chair. "I guess I had to get this Marshaling thing out of my system. Time got away from me." Giving her a pointed look, he continued. "And I didn't think you'd be waiting around, so no big hurry. And like I said, I wouldn't blame you."

"Well," she shrugged. "I haven't been idle. Keeping

busy helps. Between the miners, cattlemen, and the soiled doves next door, I keep busy." After a pause, she said, "I should thank you too."

"For...?"

"Waiting for me."

"How...?"

Laughing, she contemplated him a moment. "You're stuttering. And a woman can tell."

Quickly changing the subject, he asked. "Where are the girls?"

"Oh, now you think of the daughters." She sighed, looking out a window and then back at him. "They're sixteen now, and getting to the age where the men are looking at them. I don't like this town much. The only opportunities for young women are to get married and have babies. They need to have a means of making a living on their own. So I sent them back east to the boarding school and the college of nursing where I went. I've heard they're even turning out women doctors now."

"You think it's any different there? With men?"

"They watch their students closely. The girls won't like it, but too bad."

He nodded. "If you don't like the town, why did you stay?"

"Now you're being stupid." Her gaze settled on his.

When he didn't respond, she asked, "So, what's in the bag out by the door?"

"Let supper settle first. It's not pretty."

"I can't smell it from here." She rose from her chair. "So it can't be any worse than a boil on a hairy man's ass. Let's go see."

He set the oilskin bundle on the counter in the

examination room. When she unwrapped it and the skull rolled free, she drew a breath through her teeth. "Merciful God. Are you a Viking warrior, carrying around the heads of your enemies? Where did you find this?"

"Runaway Creek. Caught in some driftwood when the water went down."

She gave him a long glance. "And you see murder behind every tree."

"Well, driftwood in his case."

"Still a tree," she quipped.

Mattie turned the skull gently in her hands, her movements precise, professional. "Clean bone. No punctures or cracks, no erosion. These teeth—see? White as yours. This woman wasn't buried long." She looked at him. "If she was."

Turning the skull on its side, she pointed. "And her head was cut off, right at the base of the skull. No cut marks on the bone, so it was one blow. Takes a big, sharp knife to do that." She mused for a moment. "Or a sword."

Coble nodded. It wasn't uncommon for men to keep their sabers if they'd been in the cavalry. "How do you know it was a woman?"

"Easy. The skull is more rounded, smaller forehead and smaller, even teeth."

Coble nodded. "I figured as much."

Mattie straightened, her gaze steady. "You think this means murder."

"It would be quite a story if it were an accident. Can you imagine cutting off your own head? I think it means a story someone didn't want told."

"Could be she fell in the creek and drowned. Her

head may have accidentally got severed...somehow... shit." She sighed, wiping her hands. "You've got that look again. Same as before, when you went after the boy who killed his pa down in Baxter Springs. You see the devil in every man, Coble. Sometimes there isn't one to see."

"And sometimes there is." He reached into his pocket, drew out his small silver badge. It caught the light, dull and worn from years of use. "The judge made me keep this. Told me I'd know when to wear it again."

"He made you?" Mattie's eyes softened. "You could've hung that up for good."

"I thought I had."

She stood facing him, tears forming. "So, I've lost you again. You come breezing in here, knock off a piece, and you're ready to leave?"

"Hey, I still have skid marks from you dragging me." His arms went around her waist, pulling her to him. "And you have not lost me. Not anymore, and not again. I'm at the ranch permanently." He sighed. "Although I may have to clean up a few things."

Shouting interrupted the moment, and women screamed from next door. It took them less than a minute to leave the clinic and move through the doors of the club.

As they entered, they saw Amos standing in front of a girl as if shielding her from someone. To their left, a gun barked and Amos flinched, blood spurting from his shoulder.

Deputy Joseph Thibodeaux lined up his pistol for a second shot.

"He's not armed," Coble shouted, reaching for his gun.

Next to him, a gun went off, and the deputy's revolver went flying, leaving him cursing and holding his wrist.

Handing him her small pistol, Mattie went rushing toward Amos. Coble smiled, knowing she didn't want to put that hot barrel back in her dress pocket.

Coble gestured with his gun toward the door. "Get out, Deputy. That would have been murder. As it is, I'll fill out an assault warrant with the sheriff."

"You don't have authority here. None. You're just an over-the-hill ex-marshal."

Smiling, Coble said, "Well, for now, I have a gun, and you have a sore wrist. That's all the authority I need."

"This ain't over." The deputy gave Coble a menacing look.

He watched as the man stomped out the door and then turned to help Mattie take Amos next door, praying the giant wouldn't fall down. It'd take four men to get him up.

They got Amos inside the clinic and onto the table. Sitting up, he was too tall for Mattie to see the wound, so they had him lie down, thankful the table was heavy oak.

After poking and prodding a moment, Mattie said, "Well, it's a good thing Tibby uses a 36-caliber Navy gun. A .45 would have blown out your shoulder."

"Yes, ma'am. Lucky."

Mattie was brandishing a thin set of forceps. "This will hurt."

To distract the man, Coble asked. "Why'd he shoot you?"

"One woman who works upstairs has a daughter, about fourteen, I guess. He was after her." Amos grunted as Mattie pulled out the slug.

"I've seen what he does to women," Amos continued. "He likes to hurt them."

Coble shook his head. "Is that the only way she can support her daughter? Turning tricks?"

Mattie answered. "Some of them think that, even though they are mistaken."

Finished dressing the wound, she continued, "All done, Amos. Keep that clean, and I'll check it tomorrow."

"Thank you, ma'am."

By the time Amos left, it was close to sundown in a quiet town unused to violence.

"You'll spend the night?" Mattie was clinging to Coble's arm.

"Of course," he said. "Although you should prepare. It may become a habit."

"I'll chance it."

Chapter Twelve

Mattie, hair tousled, recumbent on twisted sheets, stretched to her full length, watching Coble get dressed in the early morning light.

"Dare I hope we can do this again? You're not running away, are you?"

He leaned over and kissed her. "If I run, it won't be so far you can't catch me. Right now, I'm looking to make some coffee...maybe take you out to breakfast if there's an eatery around."

She sat up, reaching for a robe. Glancing in the mirror, she recoiled. "Ugh. It'll take me a bit to get presentable. Can you wait a while?"

"Hence, making coffee first. Take your time. We've got all day."

The sound of a wagon's brakes squealing on wheels came from outside, along with a shout, "Whoa up there!"

"I'd swear that sounds like War Eagle." Coble walked toward a window but couldn't see out to the front of the building. He'd left them at the ranch. There were plenty of repairs to make and, after their argument, he wasn't sure War Eagle wanted to speak to him.

"Who?" Mattie bustled around, throwing clothes on while running fingers through her hair.

"I have friends, Mattie. Remember the men assigned to me as trackers? They're good men, and my partners now."

Exiting the living quarters, Coble moved toward the front door. He opened it just as String Bean knocked.

Was the entire world awake for this parade? To his left, he saw Amos hustling toward them, throwing on a shirt, the white bandage a solid contrast against his skin.

Glancing to his right, the ever-present Deputy Tibby strolled toward them with a curious look on his face. He noticed the deputy's hand brushing against the butt of a new pistol, his last one ruined by Mattie the previous evening.

Coble stepped outside with palms raised toward the two men approaching. "It's alright. These are friends."

Glancing back at Mattie, he said, "Mattie, this is String Bean Guiterrez. On the wagon are War Eagle Parker and our housekeeper, Adelina Morrow."

The deputy laughed. "Housekeeper? An unmarried woman living with three men? That's what you call that? Housekeeping?"

Tibby found himself slammed against the building. Coble lifted the man's revolver and tossed it to the street. "You will apologize to the young lady or start losing body parts."

Struggling for a moment, Tibby finally relaxed. Finding his feet on the boardwalk, he shook off Coble's hold and turned to Adelina. "My apologies, ma'am. I'm sure I'm mistaken."

Turning a malevolent gaze toward Coble, he said, "I won't forget this."

"That's twice you've told me you won't forget. Do you have memory problems?" Coble watched the man for a moment before turning away.

He directed his gaze at War Eagle. "And why is Adelina here? What's happened?"

String Bean whipped his hat off. "Pleased to meet you, Miss Mattie." He gave Deputy Tibby a long glance and then turned to Coble. "We got raided last night."

"Dammit," Coble sighed. "All right, how about y'all come inside. I have coffee on, and you can tell me what happened."

War Eagle was getting down from the wagon to retrieve his horse tied to the back of the wagon. Glancing at the county deputy with disgust, he kicked his pistol farther down the street before replying, "No time, Coble. We tracked them back to a cabin. Since there's three or four of them, we thought it best to come and get you."

"Makes sense. Glad you did. Now, circle back to Adelina?"

Whirling around, War Eagle said, "It ain't safe out there. They shot up the house and shot out some windows. I figured it was better for us all to stick together."

Glancing between the two of them, Coble

surmised there was something serious between them. Seeing String Bean's smirk, he was sure of it.

Deputy Thibodeaux came back after retrieving his gun and stepped up close to them. "Was anything stolen? Maybe it was some old enemies of yours?"

"They stole our draft animals and riding stock we had in the corrals, plus a small wagon. It was lucky we had more than one corral and had our personal animals stashed behind the house."

Tibby turned to Coble. "You need to report this to the sheriff before running off on your own. I'm the law in this county. You're just a used-to-be marshal and have no authority here."

"You keep saying that." Was the deputy suddenly interested in doing his job?

Watching the man walking away, Coble shook his head and turned to the small group. "Amos, would you do me a favor and stay with the ladies while we talk to the sheriff?"

"Of course," the big man said. "Won't do no good, though. Sheriff ain't left town since Moses was a pup."

"We'll see about that." Moving toward the street, he stopped and then turned back. "Amos, do you own a gun?"

"I do not."

Coble's shoulders slumped. "Great. New plan. War Eagle, you stay with Amos and the ladies. String Bean can come with me to the sheriff's office."

As Adelina was getting down from the wagon, Mattie asked. "Why the concern, Coble? It's not like we're helpless."

"Dunno, it's just a feeling. There's too much going on. I don't trust that deputy, and I don't know this sheriff. We have bones showing up in our creek, and our ranch gets marauded."

"Marauded?" String Bean turned to War Eagle. "We got marauded?"

"It didn't feel like they marauded us, felt sorta like a raid. Marauded is a lot worse."

Mattie rolled her eyes, glancing at Coble. "How about we all step inside for now? I'll stir up some eggs and bacon." She held out her hand to Adelina. "You must be tired from such a trying night." She continued, "And as for you, Coble, I don't know why you mistrust Deputy Thibodeaux so much. After all, you just met him."

Moving through the door after the others had gone inside, he replied, "Well, he shot Amos, an unarmed man. That's one thing. I just don't like him."

"So he's a little quick on the shoot." She gave him a pointed look. "I know several who are the same. He may be a bad man, but I don't know that he's crooked."

He stopped and looked at her. Being a bad man could mean many things. It could mean a wicked man who did bad things, like murder and robbery. Or, it could mean he was a man you left alone because he was dangerous to tangle with. In that context, Coble and his friends were bad. He had to wonder about Mattie's definition of this.

After a quick meal, Coble and String Bean walked to the sheriff's office. The sign outside read Barton County Sheriff. The man inside looked like a fat man in an undersized chair. He didn't get up, just waved them forward.

"Someone raided my ranch last night and stole some horses and a wagon."

The man pulled a tablet toward him on the desk. "I'll make a report on that. And you'd be?"

"Coble Bray."

"Ah, nice to meet you, Mr. Bray." He gave a politician's smile, full of teeth and throwaway promises. "I'm Dennis Springer, Barton County Sheriff." The man nodded, dropping his pencil. "MC said you'd be coming around."

Coble looked surprised. "You mean he knew we'd have horses stolen?"

"Nope." Springer laughed at that. "That's funny. He did the deal on your ranch and then stopped by to say you'd be around. The whole thing is much ado about nothing, I'm thinking."

Glancing at String Bean, Coble returned his gaze to the sheriff, a fat man too comfortable in his chair. "And what would that be?"

Springer waved a hand. "Some of his kinfolk are missing. Probably just pulled up stakes and left. People do that all the time. There's no law that says you have to tell anyone when you leave, or where you're going. Plenty of settlers get cold feet and turn back."

"I've got human bones turning up in Runaway Creek that tell a different story."

The sheriff shrugged. "Could be anything. Things happen."

"That's it? Case closed?" Finally, Coble moved toward the door. Disgusted, he turned back. "What about the horse thieves?"

"Deputy Thibodeaux takes care of things out in the county."

"We told him already. He said to tell you. Seems like that's a waste of time. Is he your only deputy?" Coble asked.

"All I need. Good day, sir." He gave Coble a dismissive look and then turned his attention to the papers on his desk.

"Did you know your deputy shot an unarmed man yesterday?"

Springer paused a moment. "Amos? I heard about that. The man doesn't know his place. He's a bouncer for hire and should do as he is told. He was standing in the way."

"Of what?"

That finally got a hard look from the sheriff. "That's not my concern, Mr. Bray. Or yours."

"There is one other thing you should know," Coble said. Taking the large US Marshal's badge from his pocket, he tossed it on the table.

"We found the judge's brother dredged up in Runaway Creek. He was in a casket. There's no way of telling how he died. I'll leave that up to you and the judge. Sounds like you need to be looking for the marshal's wife." He paused. "My opinion, of course."

Springer fingered the badge, putting on reading glasses to read the inscription. "I'll contact him. Maybe this will get him off my back. Natural causes, you say?"

Coble shook his head. "I didn't say, but people falling from ill intent don't usually wind up in a well-made wooden box."

String Bean glanced at Coble. "There must have been a lack of intrigue in your past life."

THEY'D JUST RETURNED to the clinic and waited as Mattie filled coffee cups for them. War Eagle was sitting on a bench in close conversation with Adelina while Amos was weight testing a small three-legged stool by the door. The odds were about even that the big man would be on the floor soon.

The door opened, and Deputy Thibodeaux filled the frame with a clutch of daisies in his left hand, a grin easy on his face. "Good morning again, Miss Hurst, Marshal Bray." He looked around the room. "All of y'all."

Coble tensed, one hand resting near his gun belt. This was an unexpected turnaround, bordering on strange.

Thibodeaux tipped his hat toward Mattie. "I see you're still entertaining guests and thought I'd check that everything was...peaceful."

"It is," Mattie said, voice cool. "Very peaceful. No need to fuss."

Coble studied him. "Do you make a habit of calling on ladies with flowers in hand this early in the morning, especially one you've already seen today?"

Thibodeaux smiled, slow. "Only the ones worth calling on. She's a fine lady, don't you think?" He turned his attention to the skull lying on the counter, feigning surprise worthy of an actor on stage. "Is this what has you all excited? A piece of bone?"

Mattie's chin lifted. "A woman's skull. Found in Runaway Creek. I'd think that would interest you."

Thibodeaux chuckled softly. "Could've been there for years. This country's full of ghosts and old bones. No sense digging them up."

Coble said nothing, but his eyes stayed on the deputy—watching, measuring.

The deputy turned and briefly met his gaze with a small smile.

Smiling back, Coble's fingers brushed the worn walnut butt of his pistol. Games were afoot. The players acknowledged each other.

After Thibodeaux left, strangely with flowers still in hand, the room felt smaller somehow, the fire hotter. Adrenaline kept his heart pumping fast, refusing to slow down.

"You don't like him." Mattie's voice was steady, bereft of emotion.

He gave her a curious gaze, eyebrows raised. "And you do?"

Shrugging, Mattie looked at him. "Doesn't matter. He has no foothold here. You think he's mixed up in this?"

"I don't know yet," Coble said. "I'm not even sure what is going on. Not yet. But I've seen that look in a man's eyes before. It never meant peace."

He abruptly turned to the rest of the group. "Amos, what do you know about farming?"

The man looked up, startled. "I grew up with it."

"It has occurred to me I don't want a big, sprawling ranch. Those are better suited to western Kansas. What we need is something smaller with a few horses, some cattle for beef, goats, chickens for eggs, that kind of thing. Self-sustaining. A place to raise families."

String Bean laughed, and then did a double-take when he saw that Coble was serious. "What in hell brought that on, Boss?"

He shrugged. "It's been coming on me. Seeing War Eagle cozy up to Miss Adelina is part of it. I think we need to settle down. Maybe the good deputy is right. It's time to get on with life."

War Eagle grinned at him. "It couldn't be seeing the good deputy sniffing around your gal, could it?"

He glanced at Mattie. "I can't say that thrills me. But on the other hand, that sniffing around is usually something encouraged. So that's a question that needs to be answered."

Amos stood. "I would be happy to help, sir. I'm a fair hand at repairs, too." He looked down for a moment. "This town is not to my liking. One thing. I have a woman. She'd have to come with me."

"We'll make do, Amos. For safety, when everyone is ready, I'd like y'all to load up the wagon and go back to the ranch. We do have the room, right, Adelina?"

"I'll make sure we do." She gave him a curious glance.

He turned to Mattie, noticing her angry look for the first time. "We can load up what you need and then come back for the rest." He gave her a second glance. "If that's all right?"

"No."

Coble, mind already on horse thieves, stopped in his tracks. "What?"

"I'm not going. I have a business here. People need me. I will not run off just to play house with you. I will not. And now, you've taken away the man who does all the screening for me and offers some protection. What am I supposed to do now?"

Coble stared at her, remembering the last two nights, wondering where all that had gone, making an intuitive leap. "I guess I didn't know deputies had so much time for courting."

"You have no right to judge who I see, Coble Bray. None. You left me for three long years."

"That's all true. I'm sorry about that." He gazed out the window for a moment before he replied. "Just a word of warning. I know dead eyes when I see them, Mattie. And he has them. I guess getting flowers every morning has something to do with your decision?"

Coble glanced around the room. War Eagle and Adelina were staring at him, wide-eyed. String Bean was grinning at him, and Amos just looked uncomfortable.

Finally, he nodded. "Sorry. My apologies to all of you. Sometimes I'm a bull in a china closet and don't see what's in front of my face. Ideas hit my tongue before my mind has time to process." Coble glanced around at his silent audience. "So, we're wasting time. As they have said, the ladies can take care of themselves."

He stood straighter. "Gentlemen, if you can tear yourselves away, I'm going to recover some horses. Maybe shoot some people. Suits my mood."

Outside, the world hadn't stopped. The rain had slaked the thirst of the sun-baked ground. And it seemed nothing around him cared a whit for his opinion. Coble mounted his horse, the badge still heavy in his pocket. Such was life.

War Eagle mounted his horse. "You get what you came for with the sheriff?"

Coble nodded. "Enough to lose some sleep."

"Hell, you never sleep much anyhow. And Coble? Don't count Mattie out."

Coble looked toward the horizon, where he knew the creek wound its way through the low hills, brown and secretive. He needed to change the subject. "That water's hiding something. I mean to find out what."

"Thought you said you were through with all that. Not that I believed a word of it," War Eagle grunted. "Just don't drag the rest of us into your ghosts."

He smiled faintly, though there was no humor in it. "It isn't ghosts I'm after. It's men."

"Let's ride, then," String Bean said. "I don't enjoy getting shot at, ghosts or not."

Coble turned his horse toward the open country, the morning light cutting gold through the thinning mist—while behind him, the faint echo of a woman's laugh seemed to ride the wind. And the wonderment of a woman's hot and cold demeanor.

Chapter Thirteen

Two hours of careful riding brought them to the edge of a clearing. The sun hung high and white above the pines and hardwood, bleaching the land to stillness. Between them and the silver thread of the creek stood a small cabin, rough-hewn, leaning, more ruin than home.

The three men sat quiet in their saddles, studying it. Horses flicked their tails, ears twitching. Leather creaked. The air smelled of dust and pine pitch, and something else beneath it, faint but wrong, like an old wound not yet healed.

"I see our draft animals," String Bean said finally, his shadow reaching across the grass. "But I don't see any riding stock."

War Eagle shaded his eyes. "No smoke from the chimney. Place looks deserted." His voice was flat, carrying an edge of frustration. "We should've jumped 'em early, before they flew the coop."

Coble's eyes narrowed. He'd learned long ago that silence was its own kind of warning. "Let's not get ahead of ourselves. There could be a whole herd of folks down there just waiting for us to ride up like gawkers at a parade. You two work the edges, see if there are tracks leaving. I'll go in slow and check the house. Looks like it might fall over if I breathe on it. If you hear shots, come running."

The others nodded, wordless. Unsheathing their rifles, they split off at a slow trot, moving like men who'd seen ambushes grow from shadows. Coble sat a moment longer, letting the quiet settle around him. Then he nudged his horse down into the clearing's natural bowl.

The grass there was bent and churned. A small fire pit near the porch sent up a thin white ribbon of smoke, the remnants of a meal long gone. He swung down and crouched beside it. The ashes still held warmth, the coals hadn't gone cold. They'd poured coffee over the fire, he could smell it. But they left in a hurry, not making sure the fire was out. That much was clear. They were warned.

Tin cans littered the ground, labels half peeled by bored fingers, beans, mostly. Something white caught his eye near the porch step. He bent to pick it up. A woman's shoe, small, with the heel broken. Not the kind of thing that belonged in an outlaw camp.

He turned it in his hand, uneasy. The cabin felt wrong. Empty, but not abandoned. Like something was still in there, crouched behind the silence, waiting. For a moment, he felt like a child unwilling to go into a dark closet.

War Eagle's voice carried low from behind. "There's a trail that follows the creek," he said, easing closer. "We found one horse came this way in a hurry. Someone warned them we were coming."

Coble nodded slowly. "Yeah. I figured. From the tracks, looks like they split after that. Rode in different directions. Old trick to confuse the trail, and split us up if we try to follow. They'll meet up somewhere else."

"Who knew we were riding out here?" War Eagle asked.

String Bean reined in his jumpy horse, the animal agitated by something. "Just our group, the sheriff, and the good deputy."

Coble's jaw tightened. "Tibby didn't have time to do this before he showed up at Mattie's."

"Could've sent someone," War Eagle said.

"Maybe." Coble spat in the dust. "Makes you wonder why he showed up like that, all smiles and proper, pretty as a peacock—just so we'd know he was there?"

String Bean frowned. "You think he's that slick?"

Coble gave a small shrug. "Some of the worst evil I've seen wore an innocent face."

War Eagle snorted. "It's a damn shame I never have pencil and paper when you talk like that."

String Bean shoved him lightly, but his grin didn't reach his eyes. Together they moved toward the porch, boards creaking underfoot.

The door hung on one leather hinge, swaying when the wind breathed through. Coble stepped inside first. The smell hit him—decay, old blood, and something sweet beneath it that made his stomach knot. He pulled his bandana up, though it didn't help much.

A table leaned in one corner, with a washtub beside

it. A bed frame sagged against the far wall, mattress torn open, stuffing scattered like entrails. Flies hummed. Disturbed dust turned slowly in the light, like ash with no place to go.

String Bean stayed by the door. "This smells worse than the massacre at Adobe Walls," he mumbled. "At least there we could get upwind."

Coble's eyes caught on a pile of bedding in the corner. The shape was wrong, the surrounding silence was heavier than air. He moved closer, each step a question he already knew the answer to. A bare foot jutted from the tangle. Small, gray, still. Blood streaked up the ankle.

He crouched and peeled back the blanket. A young girl who would never grow old. Her face, what was left of it, turned away, hair matted dark. He stared for a long time, feeling that familiar cold settle in behind his ribs.

"They forgot something," he said at last.

War Eagle stepped closer, handkerchief pressed tight to his face. "No," he said. "They didn't forget. They just threw her away."

Coble didn't move. He thought of the shoe outside, of her small foot inside it, of how quickly horror became ordinary when a man saw too much. He'd promised himself once that he'd never get used to sights like this. Promises didn't always hold.

When he finally spoke, his voice was flat. "Burn this place."

"What about her?" String Bean asked, his voice thin.

Coble stared at the doorway. "She's already been in

hell," he said. "Nothing here to tell us who she was. It's the best we can do."

They stepped outside into the light. The air was better, but it didn't smell clean. They worked without talking, gathering kindling, splitting loose boards, and stacking them high. The match flared, caught, and climbed the cabin's wall like a living thing. Within minutes, the place was breathing fire.

They stood watching, faces orange in the glow. The flames found the rafters, then the roof. Smoke climbed into the pale sky, twisting as the wind turned.

"Think she was one of theirs?" War Eagle asked. "Or someone they took?"

Coble didn't answer right away. "Doesn't matter," he said finally. "She ended up here."

The fire popped, sending sparks into the air like restless spirits. The creek shimmered nearby, reflecting red.

After a while, the wind shifted, carrying the smell of burning wood and something else. A different scent beneath it—sharp, earthy, and wrong. String Bean frowned. "What's that smell?"

He started walking toward the creek, covering his nose. The others followed, slow and wary. He pushed through a tangle of willow brush...and froze.

"Good God," he whispered. He stumbled back, eyes wide. Coble and War Eagle came up beside him, steadied him to keep him from falling, and saw what stopped him.

A sinkhole had opened beside the creek, its edge slick with mud. From the center, pale fingers jutted up from the muck, reaching for nothing. The water lapped against them, slow and steady.

War Eagle's voice came hoarse. "That a hand?"

Coble nodded once. "Yeah."

For a long moment, no one spoke. The world seemed to hold still. The only noises were the fire crackling behind them and the creek softly murmuring. Coble looked around the clearing again, eyes scanning shadows, trees, everything that might hide the truth.

"Boys," he said finally, "we've got trouble here. This is pure evil."

"Like that cabin wasn't?" War Eagle exhaled, shaking his head. "Still think we oughta settle down somewhere? Get on with our lives?"

Coble turned to him. His face looked older than it had an hour ago, the lines deeper, eyes hollowed. "Yeah," he said, "I do."

War Eagle gave a short laugh that didn't sound like laughter. "Right after we wade through this mess first."

"That's right." Coble's gaze drifted to the fire, now collapsing inward. "Right after we root out whatever's going on around here."

"We should move," String Bean said. "Where there is a sinkhole, it means there are caves underneath. With water running underneath all this, the area is kinda shaky. That small hole could become something big in a hurry with more rain."

"You're right," War Eagle agreed, stepping lightly. "The same thing happens in Joplin with all the mining tunnels underneath. They never know when a street is going to drop."

They watched as the cabin fell in on itself, the roof giving way with a hollow crash. As the smoke climbed higher, black against the sky, the sun slid lower, turning the world the color of rust. The creek whispered, and the frogs sang like nothing had changed at all, until a blue heron speared one and then flew away.

Coble stood there a long while, thinking of other clearings, other hands reaching from the ground. Each one had taken a piece of him. Maybe that was the price—to keep going until there was nothing left to lose, nothing more to give.

He turned at last. "Get the horses," he said. "We'll head back to the ranch. In the morning, we find out who did this."

String Bean hesitated. "You think we'll find 'em?"

Coble watched the fire die to coals, the last of the walls falling in.

"We'll find 'em," he said. "Or they will find us."

He didn't add the rest, that finding them wouldn't be the hard part. Living with what they'd have to do next always was. The only court of law for this kind of evil would come with lead balls and gun smoke.

As the three men rode out slow, facing the sun, their horses weary, shadows stretching long behind them, the cabin burned low, smoke curling over the clearing like a shroud. The wind whispered through the trees, and somewhere behind them, the creek went on singing its same old song.

By the time the last light faded, there was nothing left but red eyes of burning coals—and the promise of reckoning in the dark.

Chapter Fourteen

A WEEK HAD PASSED SINCE THEY BURNED THE OLD cabin in the hills by Runaway Creek and found the grisly remains in the sinkhole. Coble could still smell the smoke, which seemed to be embedded in his nose. Sometimes, in restless sleep, he could hear the pop of charred timbers collapsing inward.

He knew he was thinking too much—feeling too much. But he could no more turn that off than stop breathing.

They'd ridden back to the ranch the long way, through gulches choked with silt and gullies veined with runoff. Heavy rains had scoured the land clean and washed the trails of their tracks, scrubbed the hills of clues. But the questions were still there, they just came quieter, harder to answer.

When War Eagle rode down to Lamar to collect Adelina from Mattie's place, Coble stayed behind. He'd scratched out a letter to the sheriff in pencil, neat as he could manage, detailing the location of the burned-out cabin and what they'd found among the ashes. He didn't sign his name. Just folded it once, sealed it with wax, and tucked it into War Eagle's saddlebag.

He wasn't interested in answers from men who didn't want questions.

THE MORNING FOG clung like old grief along Runaway Creek. The sun burned slowly through it, steaming the dew off the tall grass, turning the air wet and warm. Upstream, a giant blue heron screeched, wings slapping water as it lifted its ungainly body and flew to the next fishing hole.

Coble sat astride his dun mare at the edge of the bluff, hat pulled low, boots caked with red clay. Below them, the swollen creek curled like a snake through the hollow. Its waters were thick with runoff—muddy, fast, and dark. Nothing about it moved quiet. Still, it seemed to whisper things.

The roots of a half-upturned oak clawed the bank like fingers reaching for sunlight.

Behind him, War Eagle Parker rode up with a soft jingle of tack and a snort from his chestnut gelding.

"You've been staring at that bend in the creek for nearly an hour," he said. "Expecting it to talk?"

Coble didn't look at him. "It already has. Just got to listen right."

War Eagle grunted and shifted in his saddle. "You're wound tighter than a cat in a rain barrel ever since we found those bones. And don't tell me it's just the bodies. You got that look in your eyes, the one that gets men killed."

Coble finally turned his head. "You think I'm chasing shadows, worrying about nothing?"

"No, I don't." With a long sigh, War Eagle seemed to choose his words wisely. "But I think it is the sheriff's job to chase shadows. It's kind of what we agreed on, isn't it? Our job is fixing fences and keeping the herd from wandering into the gulch."

"Is that what we're doing now?"

Looking around the fields of grass, violated by the gorge cut through the hill by Runaway Creek, War Eagle's jaw twitched. "It ain't what I'd call productive, no."

"It's a curious thing," Coble said. "From what we've seen, dead men are left where they fall, but the women disappear. Somehow we're finding them in the creek, or maybe in that sinkhole. Somebody should bear witness to that."

"Jesus," War Eagle muttered, shifting again in his saddle. "You don't know they were murdered. Coulda been a bunch of people died of the cholera, dysentery, or any number of things. It happens every day."

"Really, War Eagle? That's what you're going with? You saw that girl at the cabin, and that sinkhole by the creek. How else do you think this is happening? Mattie says that skull was fresh, cut from the spine."

"Fine." War Eagle held up his hand. "I'm trying to ignore the obvious. That's how I stay sane."

Coble gave him a side glance. "I'm not sure it's working. You've been in town. Did you hear of any women going missing?"

War Eagle hesitated, then spat into the grass. "Nothing official. Heard someone say a wagon train didn't make it last spring. Sheriff blamed bad luck and water crossings."

"That same sheriff who doesn't leave his desk?"

"His deputy does. That's where he gets his information." He paused a moment. "From Tibby."

After a moment of silence, War Eagle cocked an eyebrow. "Speaking of Mattie...?"

"We are?" Coble's mouth pulled tight. "I think her message was clear enough. She scratched an itch, then moved on."

"You really believe a woman's message is ever clear?" War Eagle let out a dry laugh. "You're chasing a hell of a ghost, Coble. And now you're chasing two. I don't envy you."

"Ghosts?"

"Yeah, ghosts. Things you can't see or understand. That kind of ghost."

Coble gave his friend a disgusted look. "That deputy's been sparking her with flowers and compliments."

"While you stay out here feeling sorry for yourself." War Eagle shook his head. "And you're jealous."

"Maybe a little." Coble laughed. "I thought we'd mended our fences, and all was right with us. Doesn't seem to be the case."

"And how long were you gone before you waltzed back into her life?"

"Three years."

"Jesus, Coble. You're dumber than a stump."

"And I'm not jealous," Coble continued slowly. "I'm suspicious. He smells wrong. Like grease on old iron—slick on top, rusted through underneath."

"You don't know if she gives him the time of day."

"Don't know she doesn't."

War Eagle gazed at his friend for a moment. "I believe that's what they call willful ignorance."

THEY FOLLOWED THE CREEK NORTH, hooves squelching in soft earth. Since the high water was finally receding, they could get close to the streambed. Their distasteful job had been to drag carcasses from the water—cows, pigs, even a coyote or two. Anything smaller, they left for the fish and turtles. Their intent was to help preserve the quality of the water.

The path they traveled curved past a half-rotted cottonwood tipped over on the bank, where buzzards circled low, wings black against the cloud-bleached sky.

The smell came first, putrid and wrong. War Eagle reined in hard, covering his mouth.

"Sweet mother..."

Tangled in the driftwood below was a splash of color—a dress, once blue, now bleached and ripped, caught in the roots like a flag of surrender. Pale bones jutted from the fabric, tangled and half-buried in the silt. One arm lay curled as if it had tried to reach something before the end.

"I'm tired of this," Coble muttered as he slid down from his horse and crouched at the edge. Embroidery still showed faintly at the hem of the dress, white daisies and yellow knots that might have been stars.

"We're all tired of it, Coble. No matter what the reason is. Somehow, bodies are being dumped in the creek. If nothing else, it ruins the water."

"See, the cloth's new. This isn't an old death," Coble said. "Whoever she was, she died just before the rains."

War Eagle dismounted beside him, quiet now. He crossed himself. "You gonna tell the sheriff?"

"Yeah," Coble said, still staring at the bones. "After we dig a grave. Rain's left the ground soft—won't take us long."

THAT EVENING, the wind changed. Dust came on the breeze, pale and fine, a reminder of the parched land to the west. When they rode back into the yard, the sun was a rust-colored disc sinking into the hills.

Inside the bunkhouse, String Bean Gutiérrez leaned back in a chair with one boot on the wall, whittling a twig to a point. He looked up, caught the expressions on their faces, and stilled his knife.

"Hell," he said, "I've only been gone two days. What have you done now?"

Coble stuffed his gloves in a back pocket. War Eagle went straight for the coffeepot, poured two mugs that looked like they'd been brewed with axle grease.

"You two look like men who drank Bitterroot on a dare," String Bean continued.

"Maybe we did," War Eagle muttered.

String Bean set down his knife. "What happened?"

Coble pulled out a stool and sat. "Have you been up on the north trail?"

"Yeah. Near enough."

"See any wagon remnants?"

"Just one. Burned out. Looked old—nothing recent."

Coble nodded slowly. "Same story we're seeing. Bones in the creek, burned campsites. But these bones are fresh. Someone is still dumping bodies. They're just not as careful as before."

String Bean whistled, low and sharp. "Do you think Thibodeaux is involved?"

Coble looked out the dark window. His voice was quiet. "It's possible. I think he's got men riding for him. Hired guns without names. Have you ever met a man with no history? No one seems to know where he came from."

"Only once. Shot me in the leg and didn't even stick around to check."

"Then you know the kind," Coble said.

"Then, the big question is why? Is there someone running around just looking for women? Maybe they're just a by-product...considered an extra? We don't know."

Coble nodded and then shrugged. "If we find where they are selling what they steal, we'll be closer to figuring all this out."

War Eagle leaned against the doorframe. "You've still got nothing solid. Intuition doesn't hold in court."

"I'm not going to court," Coble said. "Men like these don't go looking for a lawyer. I'm going to town tomorrow."

LATER, when the others had turned in, War Eagle

lingered near the door. "You're stirring up hornets, Coble. That deputy's got friends."

"So did the devil," Coble said, standing. "Didn't stop his fall."

Outside, the prairie wind picked up, carrying the smell of rain and old earth from the creek bottom. Somewhere in the dark, a coyote yipped once and went silent.

Coble listened for a long time, hand resting on the badge in his pocket. It was cold as bones in the river.

Tomorrow, he'd ride into town.

And Joseph Thibodeaux would know someone was listening.

Chapter Fifteen

MATTIE SAT BEHIND HER DESK, ONE BOOT BRACED against the chair leg, pencil scratching slowly across the page. The window was partly open, and the late morning breeze curled the edge of her notes. She blew a stray lock of hair out of her face, flipped a page, and scribbled down:

Patient: Tom Denny. Laceration to forearm, treated with carbolic acid and six stitches. Told him to lay off the whiskey and rest, which means I'll see him again inside two days, likely bleeding again.

She added a line beneath it, *New vial of carbolic needed*, and underlined it twice.

The floor creaked outside.

Mattie didn't look up at first. She knew the sound of *those* boots—slow, showy, heels polished to click louder than they should. She sighed.

When she glanced toward the doorway, Amos filled the frame, like a boulder rolled there to block the sun. Beyond him, the black shine of the boots stood firmly on the boardwalk, waiting.

"Let him in, Amos," she said without enthusiasm, rubbing the bridge of her nose.

Amos didn't move aside. Instead, he stepped *into* the room and folded his arms.

Deputy Thibodeaux stomped in a heartbeat later, all confidence and cologne. He wore pinstriped black trousers and a crisp white shirt with a high collar. A black vest hugged his chest, and the silver star pinned over it caught the light as if begging to be admired. Everything about him seemed polished, pressed, or perfumed.

"Are you injured, Deputy? Sick, maybe?" Mattie asked flatly. She didn't bother to smile.

"Only my pride, maybe." His tone was warm as bourbon—smooth, practiced, just shy of charming. "I was just checking on you. Making sure you're well cared for."

Mattie gave a tight smile that didn't reach her eyes. "I'm doing fine. Healthy as ever."

He tilted his head, trying on a softer expression. "You're all alone. This town eats good women alive. A lady like you deserves better."

"I'm not alone." She nodded slightly toward Amos. "And I assure you, I've had worse neighbors than dust and disease."

He chuckled, but his eyes didn't move. They stayed locked on her face—flat, glassy, unreadable. "You deserve more than what you've got, Mattie. I could provide that for you."

She sighed and stood up, placing both hands on her desk. "Deputy, I've said no. Repeatedly. There is nothing here for you. And there never will be."

His smile faded. He straightened his back like

someone about to make a speech or pull a pistol. "You really mean that?"

"I do. I'm not one to play hard-to-get. Most everyone will tell you I always speak my mind, and it's a rare day that I stray from the truth. I expect you to honor that." Her hand drifted toward her pocket pistol, just in case.

He stood still for a moment longer, and then, without a word, turned on his heel.

At the door, he cast a last glare at Amos. It wasn't angry, it was *cold*, like he was memorizing the shape of the big man's throat.

Once the deputy had vanished, Amos closed the door gently and turned around. "I don't like that man."

Mattie looked up with a grim smile. "Of course not. He shot you."

Amos grunted. "And I don't think he's done with me, either. Or you. He looks at people as if they're nothing. Like he's already decided who gets to keep breathing."

Mattie studied his face. "Do you have a point, or is this just foreboding small talk?"

"I think he's touched," Amos said. "He's like a dangerous dog. Don't bark, don't warn...just bites."

Mattie turned back to her journal and made a note. *Deputy visited again. Persistent. Eyes dead like Coble said. Worrisome.*

She kept her voice level. "Let me guess. You think I ought to pack up and run off to the ranch."

"Wouldn't hurt," Amos said, folding his arms again. "Coble's got men. Guns. Fences. Hell, even beds."

She gave him a serious look. "You're afraid of Tibby, aren't you?"

"Not in a fair fight," Amos replied. "But it won't be fair. When he comes for you, he'll come at dusk or dawn. And he'll shoot me first, just like swatting a fly. I've got a feeling he'll keep shooting until I'm down."

Mattie turned in her chair, looking him full in the face. "Why stay then? Coble offered you a place to live and a job. You should go."

Amos shrugged. "My place is here. Far as I'm concerned, it's not loyalty. Its purpose."

"You're a brave man, Amos."

He gave her a crooked grin. "I'll take brave over smart." He paused. "Why don't you go?" he asked. "That man wants you, and I've seen how you look at him."

"You're a giant romantic, you know that?" She shook her head. Her reasons were getting weaker. She returned to his question. "Pride, I guess. I don't like to be run off from anything."

When he stepped out, she turned back to the journal, flipping backward through a half dozen pages. Every time Thibodeaux had visited, she'd made a note. They were becoming more frequent. More personal.

And Coble...well, that was a different mess entirely. She'd wanted to explain herself after he left, to tell him it had meant nothing, to talk, to explain. But he didn't wait. He just left.

Still, she'd mend that fence, eventually.

She just hoped he'd still be standing on the other side of it when she got there.

Across town, Deputy Thibodeaux pushed open the door of the sheriff's office with more force than was strictly necessary.

Sheriff Springer looked up from his desk with surprise and a half-finished sandwich in hand. "Something wrong?"

"I'll be gone a couple of days," Tibby said, adjusting his vest. "Got to check into a few things."

"What things?" Springer set his beef sandwich down, suddenly alert.

Tibby's jaw clenched. "Things that are none of your concern."

The sheriff slumped a bit. "Right. Fine. You, uh... have a good trip."

Tibby's lip curled, then he turned and left without another word.

Outside town, just beyond the rise where the road split east toward Mindenmines, three men lounged beneath a cottonwood tree. They sat on their horses like men who'd done it all their lives, quiet, confident, slow to smile.

Beside them, three pack animals stood tethered to a low fence, weighed down with saddlebags and crates. Inside the packs were silverware, trinkets, heirloom quilts, bottles of whiskey, all loot lifted from burned-out wagons and vanished travelers. No one would miss what no one remembered.

Tibby rode up and nodded once. "Let's ride."

The three men turned their horses with lazy precision.

"We should make it to Mindenmines by nightfall," Tibby said, looking out across the wide, sun-drenched prairie. "We trade right, we ride hard, and no names. Clear?"

They nodded.

"And if anybody asks," he said, pulling gloves onto his hands, "we're horse traders. Simple folk. Keep your mouths shut and let me do the talking."

He glanced back once toward town, stuffing his deputy sheriff star into a pocket.

Mattie would come around eventually. Or she'd disappear like the others. Either way, he'd deal with her. In the meantime, there were women in Mindenmines who were more willing...for the right price.

He kicked his horse forward, and the group moved west, dust rising behind them.

THEY REACHED Mindenmines just after dusk.

The town squatted low against the horizon, huddled like a secret. Smoke curled from chimneys, lifting slowly in the cooling air. Lanterns flickered behind grimy windows. The streets were muddy, packed with wheel ruts and old boot prints, and the air stank faintly of coal dust and something burned that didn't come from any fire meant for warmth.

Tibby and his three men rode in without slowing. No salutes. No greetings. Just four shadows moving through the dying light.

The town hadn't changed since the last time he'd been through. One main street. Two saloons. An open-air blacksmith shop. A general store that did more business out the back than the front. He could smell whiskey, and coal dust, and gun oil.

As they passed the old stone church, now leaning like a drunk against time, one horse let out a nervous snort. Tibby didn't look up. He was focused on the mercantile.

The bell above the door jangled as Tibby entered. The place was empty, save for a man behind the counter counting tobacco tins into a crate.

"Hello, Ward," Tibby said. "Thought you'd be over tending bar."

The man looked up, startled. "Tibby. I don't see you much these days."

"I brought a few trade items." Tibby pointed outside. His men had already begun unloading the packs.

Ward wiped his hands on a rag and followed outside. "Same as last time?"

Tibby grinned. "Better."

They stepped out the back door, where the crates were being opened one by one. Inside, a mix of items that made no sense together unless you knew the source—ladies' gloves, child-sized boots, a locket with initials etched in cursive. Blood still crusted the inside of one silver sugar bowl.

Ward nodded slowly. "You want cash or trade?"

"Both." Tibby's voice was flat. "And anything in newsprint. Especially anything about disappearances. We'll want mostly cash and women for the night."

"Might be hard to get women after the last time you were here."

Tibby snorted. "That kind of woman doesn't care if you rough them up a bit."

Ward's eyes narrowed. "Back to the newspaper. You expect something to hit print?"

"I expect a man to be prepared," Tibby said.

One of the men opened a crate with three bolts of cloth. Another unwrapped a half-broken music box that still played the first few notes of *Red River Valley* before jamming up.

Ward sucked in a breath. "You didn't get these from a trader. Not unless he was already cold."

Tibby leaned in, smile gone. "Do I look like I want questions from you? Are you getting skittish all of a sudden?"

Ward stepped back. "No, sir. You look like you want whiskey and your business done quick."

"Now we understand each other."

By the time they finished, the sky had gone black. A few drunks stumbled out of the Coal Dust Saloon, laughing too loud, one dragging a broken fiddle. Tibby watched them for a moment.

Then he turned to his men. "You got the night. We ride at daylight. If I hear about any talking out of turn, we'll bury you here."

"Where are we going next?"

"Back to Runaway Creek," Tibby said. "We have work to do there."

THE KEROSENE LAMP hissed softly on her desk, casting a pool of golden light across the pages. Mattie dipped the nib of her pen in ink, then hesitated. Her eyes lingered on the name she'd just written. *Thibodeaux, visit #6.*

She stared at it for a long while, then underlined it.

Outside, wind whispered through the alley. She

heard the wooden slats of the fence rattle like loose teeth.

She pushed the journal aside, lost in thought.

Footsteps sounded behind her.

"Amos?" she called without turning.

"Nope," said a familiar voice, one she hadn't expected at this hour.

Joanne, her sometime helper, stood in the doorway, arms crossed, hair pinned back tight. She looked tired but determined. "You got tea?"

Mattie blinked, then smiled. "Of course. You look like hell."

"You should see the other woman," Joanne muttered, stepping inside. "I swear, they're worse than men."

They settled at the small table near the stove, with the tea steeping between them.

"You come about Tibby?" Mattie asked.

"People talk. I came because Coble's stirring up things that don't like being stirred. And I know what kind of men follow Tibby Thibodeaux."

Mattie sipped her tea. "So do I."

Joanne leaned forward. "I saw one of them last week. Watched him drag a crate into the back of the freight office. No manifest. No questions. Like they owned the whole damn place."

"They don't need ownership. They've got fear."

Joanne looked at the journal. "You still writing everything down?"

Mattie nodded. "Every visit. Every look. Every time he tries to pretend it's just kindness."

Joanne met her gaze. "That might be the only

proof anyone will ever have if something happens to you."

Mattie's mouth tightened. "I won't let it get that far."

"You might not get a say." Joanne didn't smile, her serious gaze locked on Mattie.

They sat in silence for a moment as the wind picked up, making the walls groan. In the distance, a dog barked—then went silent, hushed by a man shouting at it.

"Let me know if you hear anything else, Joanne. I might need a head start."

The woman chuckled. She'd seen the bad side of too many men and women to have any faith in what they might, or might not, do.

She shook her head. "What you need is to swallow your pride and get the hell out of here. Bad things are going to happen."

Chapter Sixteen

IT WAS LATE EVENING BEFORE COBLE RODE INTO Lamar. The sky had bled itself into rust and gray, and the wind smelled of dust and the coming rain. He passed the blacksmith's, the post office, the shuttered storefronts, each with a lamp burning behind thin curtains. People here were afraid of the dark, and maybe they were right to be.

On a whim, or maybe an old reflex that whispered *delay the hard thing,* he tied his horse in front of the Gentleman's Club. He figured a drink might sand down the edges before he went to see Mattie. As much as he wanted to see her, he dreaded the confrontation. He knew the words he wanted to say... just not the order to put them.

Inside, the place was low on light and high on lies. Tobacco smoke hung thick enough to chew. The piano player was slow and tired, and laughter came from throats that didn't mean it.

Coble leaned on the bar, letting the whiskey burn

in slow turns. He wasn't here for the taste. It just gave his hands something to do.

A figure stepped up beside him. He turned, ready to tell her he wasn't interested, but stopped short.

"Aren't you Joanne, the girl who helps next door at the clinic?"

She smiled thinly. "Sometimes. When she needs me. After sundown, though, I work here. Amos and me both."

"Hard way to make a living."

"Don't I know it." She shrugged, a gesture that said she'd stopped measuring the weight of things long ago. "I only hustle drinks for tips. It's not the worst thing if I stay close to the poker tables. Men seem to tip better when they're losing at cards."

He nodded and then looked away. "Well, good luck with that."

She didn't move. "I need a word, if you don't mind."

"Concerning?" At second glance, she was a small woman, well put together, but a little past her prime. She had the look of someone with experience beyond her years, with a hard expression and granite eyes.

Her voice softened. "Mattie."

The sound of her name hit him in the ribs. He said nothing, watching closely.

Joanne drew a long breath, the words heavy in her throat. "That girl loves you, Coble. You're killing her."

He and Mattie were both well-traveled, in years and experience. He swallowed hard, staring into the amber in his glass. "We're too old for the romance that comes from the new books and magazines we see. And it seems to me she's the one pushing away. I fear she's taken a shine to Tibby."

Joanne snorted. "A shine? She's terrified of him. We all are. That man's not right in the head. The only difference is she's tough as nails and better at pretending she's not afraid."

His glance sharpened. Unbidden, his hand brushed the butt of his pistol. "Has he hurt her?"

"Not yet." Her voice dropped. "But he controls this town, Coble. You know it's coming. He's got a way of circling what he wants till it's too tired to fight."

Coble's jaw tightened. "You sure?"

"As sure as I am of the drink in your hand." She shook her head. "But she hasn't seen the world like I have."

"She might have seen more than you think." He turned to look at Joanne then, and for a moment, she looked almost sorry for him.

"You got a choice, Coble," she said. "Get her out of here. Or stop Tibby before he takes her."

He didn't answer. She waited, shrugged, and then walked away, her skirts brushing against men who dared to think she might be theirs for the night.

The piano started another tune, softer, sadder, if that was possible. Coble thought of the bones out at Runaway Creek, the way they turned pale in the moonlight, proof of people who thought they had more time on this earth than they did.

He was ready to leave when the bartender spoke while polishing a glass.

"You used to wear a badge, right?"

"Used to." Coble gave him a curious glance, wondering where he'd seen the man before.

The man leaned closer, his voice a rasp. "Fella came through last week. Drunker than sin. Talking about families going missing, wagons stripped, cattle run off. He laughed when he said it was easy money."

"Sounds like something the sheriff should know."

The bartender gave a humorless laugh. "Sheriff Springer is stuck in his chair. The only time he leaves it is for a free meal or whiskey. Tibby runs this county. Everyone knows that."

"Anyone specific missing that you know of? Names?" Coble asked.

"Sorry"—the man turned away—"just rumors."

"Thanks for the information." Coble stood there for a long moment, thinking how useless the information was, then tipped his hat and walked out. The street was empty, with a quietness that was peaceful, or ominous, depending on the expectations of the people you knew.

THE CLINIC LIGHT STILL BURNED, faint and yellow through the curtains. He knocked softly. No answer. He was turning away when the door opened.

Mattie stood there, hair down, eyes sharp despite the weariness in them.

"Well, hey, it's the rancher. Are you coming in, or just knocking on doors to run away like the kids do?"

Hesitating, he asked. "Do you want me to?"

"Dammit, Coble." She turned away, leaving the door open.

He followed her in, shutting and locking the door behind him. The smell of clean linen and herbs met the dust and whiskey on his shirt, two worlds that didn't belong in the same room.

Leaning against the counter, she crossed her arms. "Well? What's on your mind? I can smell the saloon on you. Did you get turned down there?"

"I'm not sure I'll ever get used to that smart mouth of yours. And for your information, all I had was interesting conversation." He managed a smile that struggled to reach his eyes. "I'm sorry I walked away the other day. I just figured there wasn't much point in arguing when your mind is made up."

She softened a little. "Funny. To men, it's arguing. For women, it's talking things out. That's what couples do when they care for each other."

"Couples?" He smiled at her.

The lamplight softened her face, but her eyes stayed wary. "I don't know. You still chasing bones?"

Things were never simple. For Mattie, things were black or white, yes or no. It seemed his life often seemed to run along the line between the two. He often thought the easy days were always behind him, with hope for the future, a distant dream. All he was doing now was stacking days.

"Not bones, Mattie. Men. Someone who takes all the hopes and dreams of a young girl and squeezes the life out of it." Noticing her expression, he continued, "Is that talking enough for you?"

She sighed, rubbing her temples. "That is what stands between us, Coble. Don't you see that? There's always another man to hunt, murder to solve, or grave to dig. You can't stop who you are."

He stepped closer, lowering his voice, pleading without realizing it. "If I stop, good people die."

"Most are dead already, you're just picking up the pieces." She turned away from him, staring at the dark window. "Good people are going to die anyway. And the bad ones find new towns to prey on, keep doing what they do."

The silence between them was thick.

He said, "So where does that leave us, Mattie? You can't keep pulling me in while pushing me away."

"I'm taking care of myself, staying alive. That's about all I can promise." After a long pause, she said with a tremulous voice, "You staying the night?"

"Only if I'm wanted." He couldn't keep the sadness from his voice, his thoughts.

Her voice turned soft, brittle as frost. "It's not about the wanting, Coble. I've never wanted anyone like I want you. It's living with when you ride away. The fear you won't come back."

He should've left then, and spared them both the ache. But when she turned away, her shoulders trembling with the weight of things unsaid, he crossed the space between them. His hands found her waist, and for a long moment she didn't move. Then she leaned back against him, and all the fight went out of her.

Her soft voice breathed it all. "Dammit, Coble."

Their kiss wasn't tender, but full of want and need, survival. A desperate trade of warmth against the ugliness outside. When she pulled away, her eyes shone with something closer to fear than love. "This won't fix us," she whispered.

He nodded. "Didn't think it would. Maybe put a bandage on it for now."

Neither of them stepped apart.

LATER, when the lamplight burned low and her breathing steadied beside him, Coble lay awake, staring at the ceiling. Rain had started outside again, a thin, steady fall tapping the window like restless fingers. It seemed to rain every day now.

He thought of Joanne's words. Of Tibby's men, the ones who stripped wagons and left nothing but silence and death behind. Of a man with a scar running from cheek to collarbone.

He thought of how fear never slept in Lamar, it just changed faces.

By dawn, he was gone. Left before she woke, the bed still warm, the world already colder.

He didn't leave a note. It's hard to put words to things you haven't figured out. The wind carried the smell of wet earth, and somewhere behind him, a woman stood at a window, watching him disappear.

MATTIE LEANED AGAINST THE WINDOWSILL, arms folded tight against the chill. She hadn't meant to watch him, but her body hadn't asked her permission. Every receding hoof fall made her heart ache.

She pressed her palm to the glass. It was cold. So was she.

Behind her, Joanne slipped in quietly, bonnet in hand. "He's gone, huh?"

Mattie didn't turn. "He always is."

She asked then. "Why are you up and about this early? Don't you ever sleep?"

Joanne hesitated, then said, "You ought to know... there's talk already. Amos said a man came through last night, asking questions."

Mattie's breath caught. "He asked about Coble?"

"He didn't say a name. Just said he was looking for an ex-marshal who lived hereabouts."

Mattie turned from the window then, eyes sharp again. "Where is this man now?"

Joanne shrugged. "He and Tibby rode out about an hour ago. Out past the river road."

Mattie gripped the counter to steady herself. "Then it's starting."

Joanne frowned. "What is?"

"Whatever Coble was looking for." She turned to look at Joanne. "He always said that if he waited long enough, evil would always look for him. They can't help themselves, it's in their nature."

"Sounds like he knows what he's talking about."

Mattie sighed, palming a tear coursing down her cheek. "He also told me that evil will start fires just to see them burn—his job is to see evil burn in that fire." She paused for a moment and then took a deep breath. "I'm scared, Joanne. More scared than I've ever been."

Outside, a wagon rolled by with its tarp flapping loose. A child's toy, a little wooden horse, tumbled out into the mud. No one stopped to pick it up.

Mattie stood in the clinic's doorway, eyes on the horizon. She couldn't see him, but she felt the distance between them growing wider than the plains.

"Lord help him," she whispered.

But she didn't know if she was praying for his safety...or for what he might have to do next. One would bring him back to her, the other would take one more notch from his soul. She didn't know how much he had left to give.

COBLE HADN'T GONE FAR. He never did when his gut told him something was coming. He stopped on a rise a mile outside of town, watching the horizon. The mist hadn't burned off yet, and Lamar looked small through it, small and helpless.

He reached into his coat pocket and pulled out his badge, pinning it to his shirt. A decision made, life or death.

The sound of hoofbeats behind him made his hand go to the Schofield in his belly holster. He turned slowly.

A lone rider emerged from the haze. Thin, easy in the saddle, his face was half-hidden beneath a hat brim.

The man reined up ten paces away. "Morning, Marshal." He pointed toward the badge on Coble's shirt. "I see you're advertising now."

"You got business with me?" Coble asked.

The man smiled, but there was no warmth in it. "Reckon that depends on how you define business."

Silence settled between them, broken only by the horse's breathing.

Finally, the stranger said, "Tibby says you've been asking questions that don't need answers. You're bad for business."

"Is that business murder? Stealing from good people?" Coble's thumb rested lightly on the hammer of his gun. "Maybe Tibby should do his own talking."

"I can see what you want in your eyes, Marshal. But I will not draw on you, and you can't kill me in cold blood." The man's smile faded. "Tibby will find you. Sooner than you think."

"Don't bet your life on me not killing you. I'm starting to reevaluate that notion as untenable. You got a name, something I can put on your tombstone?"

"More likely to put on a warrant. Hell, not that it matters. The name's Doyle."

Coble nodded. "Well, Doyle, you be sure to come with Tibby when he finds me. Promise me."

The man didn't move, didn't blink. He studied Coble for a second longer. "I've got a better idea. Told Tibby I'd deliver the message. Now I've done that. But I'm lighting a shuck out of here." Doyle paused for a moment. "People in town see him as a smooth as butter deputy, nice as can be. But that man's plum crazy. We had a kid with us who talked too much, and one of his henchmen, Scottie, killed him. Tibby comes back and kills Scottie. Marshal, I'm no saint, done enough to hang for, twice over. But I've had enough."

After his speech, the man turned his horse and rode off, slow and deliberate, slumped in the saddle.

Coble watched him go, then turned his horse toward Runaway Creek.

Life would be simpler if he could just shoot the peckerwoods. But Doyle had him pegged right. He couldn't.

Chapter Seventeen

South of Lamar was a crossroads. The trail ran alongside the KATY Railroad. A wagon road crossed the tracks, going east toward a little German town called Lockwood and on to Springfield. The road traveled west to Fort Scott, Kansas.

Crossroads often turn into slapped-together settlements, and this one was no different. Someone hung a sign that read Jubal's Crossing. There was a general store, a dilapidated hotel, and a saloon. It was all they needed.

The cluster of buildings sat at a confluence of county lines, no one being sure who had jurisdiction over the place, so it was mostly ignored.

Tibby stood at the bar in the saloon, bar being a kind description. Three two-by-twelve rough-hewn planks were nailed across the tops of empty fifty-gallon whiskey barrels. The crowded room, ripe with sweat and smoke-filled, needed fresh air like a drowning man.

He motioned to the bartender and proprietor. "I need to hire some men."

"Good luck with that. This lot ain't much for day labor." The man looked at him. "How many and what for?"

"It'll be an easy day. There's a ranch house west of Lamar, got two, maybe three men and one woman in it. I want it gone from the face of the earth."

"Ah, that kind of labor. I've got plenty of those." The bartender gave him a long look. "Last I heard, you had men of your own, Tibby. What about them?"

Tibby shrugged. "Some met an unfortunate end, and I think another ran away. It's hard to get good help these days."

"It won't be any easier here. I'll put the word out. But I must tell you, there ain't many that want anything to do with your business. Too much death."

Tibby gave him a long look. "I appreciate your concern. When I'm through taking care of business, I'll be back to deal with you."

"I'll be here." Unimpressed and shoving a bottle toward him, the bartender said, "On the house. Just don't shoot up the place. And Tibby? We have a couple of working girls here. Do not touch them. I've got a Greener stuffed full of buckshot and six-penny nails if you do. Working women are hard to come by, and you've got a reputation."

Tibby gave him a baleful stare and then shrugged. "All right. For now."

There were other women. Besides, he wanted to stay sober for the ride to the ranch on Runaway Creek. There was a house to burn down and a marshal to kill.

THE SUN HAD SLIPPED low by the time Tibby and his hired men crested the rise east of the ranch house. Six of them rode in loose formation, silhouettes sharp against the fading light. They weren't professionals, just drifters and hard cases, men who got mean when they were bored and drunk. But Tibby didn't need good men. He just needed violent ones, and they'd mostly sobered up on the ride over.

He'd paid in silver up front and promised more when the job was done.

Below them, Runaway Creek caught the sun in its winding path like a blade of fire. The ranch house stood farther back, just past the corrals, a neatly put-together place, pale, two-storied, with smoke curling from the chimney. East of the house, a shed leaned into the wind, and the barn behind it cast a long shadow like a squat, crouching thing.

Tibby adjusted his hat and pointed toward the property. "There. That's it. I want it all gone. There's only three men and a woman. After we're done, you can have the woman for a while, but they all die."

One rider shifted, looking at Tibby doubtfully. "What'd they do?"

Tibby gave him a sharp look. "They pissed me off."

The rider looked away. The look on Tibby's face made him more sober than he wanted to be.

Tibby clicked his tongue, and the men moved toward the buildings.

COBLE STOOD on a ladder outside the barn, hammering a fresh crossbeam into place where the last storm had torn loose part of the siding from the eaves. War Eagle passed up nails in a bucket while jawing at String Bean.

String Bean had just returned from the lower pasture, a trail of dust rising behind his horse, after visiting the Myers place five miles west to look at a pair of young steers for sale. They were nothing special, just skin-and-bone yearlings with burrs in their tails.

Inside the house, Adelina snapped green beans at the table, freshly bought from a farmer north of them, humming softly to herself. War Eagle had told her he liked to hear her humming and singing. It made the house feel like a home.

The wind picked up a little, fluttering the curtain in the kitchen window.

Adelina paused.

She heard something. It was faint but wrong. Not wind, nor wagon wheels. Not cattle lowing as they bedded down for the night.

Horses on a dead run.

THEY CAME IN FAST, not in formation but like a swarm of wasps, splitting left and right as they galloped into the yard, shouting, guns raised. Tibby rode at the front, one hand loose on the reins, the other holding a sawed-off scattergun across his lap.

Coble heard the first gunshot and dropped his hammer. It clattered down the ladder, barely missing

War Eagle as he jumped the last four rungs. "War Eagle, get to the house and find cover."

They scrambled just as bullets tore through the corner of the building. Splinters flew. The horse in the pen reared up, screaming, snapping a corral rail as it bolted free.

War Eagle dove behind a pile of hedge posts, rolling to a stop and spitting dust.

"What the hell is this?" he growled.

String Bean made it to the porch of the ranch house, firing quickly with his Winchester, shooting in the general direction of the raiders. Ducking behind the porch columns, he yelled into the house.

"Adelina, get on the floor."

INSIDE, Adelina dropped the bowl of beans, which scattered like green shrapnel. She grabbed the pistol hidden under the sink and slid across the floorboards behind the protection of the iron stove, heart hammering in her throat.

OUTSIDE, the riders circled the yard, firing into the windows and door, waving torches. One rider peeled off toward the barn, but a bullet from Coble dropped him before he made it twenty feet.

Tibby dismounted behind the smokehouse and stepped forward calmly, almost leisurely, shotgun slung over one arm. He called out over the noise of gunfire, "Coble Bray. I know you're here. You've been a tick on my hide long enough. Come out and we'll settle this square."

Coble ducked around the back of the barn, signaling to War Eagle with two fingers—*go left*. "Only thing square about you, Tibby," he called back, "is your head."

The comment came at a lull in the firing and drew a few laughs from the hired attackers, nervous ones.

Tibby's voice went darker. "I'm going to burn you down."

And he meant it. Already, one rider had lobbed a torch onto the shed roof. It caught fast. Old dry timber, probably with mouse nests in the rafters, welcomed the flame. The fire roared to life in seconds.

Inside the house, smoke crept under the door from a blaze starting on the back porch.

IN THE YARD, String Bean's second shot took out a man trying to torch the front of the house. The return fire tore up the siding above his head.

"We can't hold this long," he shouted. "There's too many of them."

"Then we don't," Coble said, ducking behind the water trough. "We move."

"Where?" War Eagle asked, reloading behind the hay wagon.

"Creek," Coble said. "We bait them in. Let the gorge do the killing."

War Eagle grinned. "Now you're thinking like a bastard."

They moved fast, String Bean covering their break

with another pair of shots. Coble kicked open the back door of the house while War Eagle pulled Adelina out by the arm. She was coughing, eyes watering, but she was armed and ready.

They kept their riding mounts in a separate pen behind the house. With String Bean giving covering fire, it didn't take long to saddle up.

"South to the gorge," Coble ordered. "Ride light, move fast. Stick to the shadows."

Tibby saw them moving. "Over there on the south side, boys. Don't let them reach the creek."

But it was too late.

Coble and the others rode hard and low, cutting behind the burning barn, through the outer pens, and down toward the gorge. Gunshots followed, but most went wild. Tibby and his remaining men charged after them, but the ranchers knew the land, every rise, every break in the grass.

The gorge waited.

Coble and String Bean split left and right, flanking the edge. Coble was glad they hadn't been able to put up a fence.

War Eagle dropped behind a low cedar, rifle trained. Adelina dismounted beside him, crouched low, and covered the rear.

Tibby didn't slow down.

Two of his riders came up fast and didn't see the drop until it was too late. One screamed all the way down. The other didn't make a sound.

Tibby's horse reared just at the edge, throwing him

hard. He hit the ground, rolled, came up coughing dust and blood, shotgun gone.

Coble stepped out, revolver aimed. "You have only two men left, Tibby. It's over."

Tibby laughed, blood on his teeth. "It ain't ever going to be over, Marshal. Not for us."

Coble didn't reply.

The only light came from the burning buildings, and both men were moving, firing at the same time.

Tibby coughed blood, staggered upright, holding his side. "Damn you."

Seeing a thrown revolver hurtling his way, Coble flinched...just enough. His return fire went wide.

Tibby sprinted sideways, half-falling, grabbing a riderless horse. Bullets snapped past him. He hauled himself into the saddle with raw instinct and kicked the animal hard.

String Bean fired twice at him, and missed.

War Eagle aimed carefully, but Tibby's horse veered just in time. He vanished into the trees, hunched low, bleeding, but alive.

War Eagle moved up with his arms around Adelina. "I swear, that man's got a charmed life. We must have wasted a dozen bullets on him."

"I saw blood," String Bean said. "Someone got him."

Coble sighed, holstering his pistol. "All right, that's enough. Let's go back and see what we can save. String Bean, I want you to hang around across the creek in case one of those idiots gets brave again."

"Got it, Boss."

DAWN CAME with deep blue skies, turning to streaks of red and gold. The soot-blackened survivors were too tired to notice. Luckily, the fire had burned itself out. There were only so many buckets of water one could carry from the creek.

The barn was gone. The shed, too. But the house still stood, partly smoke-blackened, half the back porch charred, but standing and livable.

String Bean, having given up sentry duty, sat on the stoop, covered in soot, sipping coffee like it was a holy thing. War Eagle limped past, carrying a blackened saddle. Coble stood in the yard, watching the first light catch on the surface of Runaway Creek.

He said nothing.

But something in the way he stood, straight-backed and jaw set, said plainly. They'd rebuild.

"We got lucky," he said.

"No," Adelina said, brushing cinders from her sleeves. "They were stupid, thinking they were fighting ordinary ranchers. Y'all are more like soldiers."

War Eagle wordlessly hugged her. They were both exhausted.

Coble looked toward the horizon, jaw set. "Tibby will be back. Next time, he won't bring amateurs."

War Eagle lifted a scorched whiskey bottle from the dirt. The cork had burned off, so he had to pry it out with his knife. He took a long, smoky drink. Adelina took it from him, knocked back a long pull, shuddered, and offered it to String Bean.

"Then we'll be ready," she said.

"That we will," Coble said. "I want all of you to concentrate on getting the house back in shape. Get rid of the burned parts, and cut firing ports into the shutters. You might offer to pay some of the farmers around here to help, especially if they have lumber to spare. But the first thing," Coble continued, "see what you can do with the bodies, especially those two that went into the gully. That'll ruin the water for some time to come if we don't pull them out of there."

"What are you going to do, Coble?" War Eagle asked. "This thing has us back on our heels a bit. We need to get ahead of it. I'm going to see if I can bust that sheriff out of his chair. Then I'll do some hunting." He glanced at their faces. "But I won't be long. The battle is more likely to be here than anywhere else."

Chapter Eighteen

Tibby rode into Lamar at dawn, half-slumped in the saddle and clinging to the pommel like a man riding through the gates of Hell half-drunk. His coat soaked through with blood on the left side, the fabric dark and stiff, his hand pressed hard to the wound like he could somehow hold the pain in with sheer will.

Having stopped at the crossroads for whiskey, all the buildings were dark. The bartender, not happy with getting rolled out of bed before dawn, took one look at his wound and shook his head. The wound was more than he wanted to tackle, especially since Tibby had talked him out of a spare pistol.

Tibby didn't bother with side roads. He came straight down the main street like he owned it.

The few early risers gave him a wide berth. One shopkeeper froze with a broom mid-sweep. A boy pumping water dropped the handle and ran.

Tibby didn't even notice. His vision had narrowed to a single building at the far end of town, a white-washed, single-story shotgun dwelling, with green shutters and a sign swinging faintly in the wind: *Medical Clinic*

The horse stopped because it had to. Tibby didn't dismount so much as slide sideways and crash to the ground. He groaned once, high and ugly, and then staggered upright, dragging himself toward the door, dripping a red trail behind him.

INSIDE, Mattie had just finished breakfast and was laying out clean gauze when she heard the thump on her porch and what sounded like a screech. The sound wasn't unfamiliar. Sometimes a man fell off his horse drunk, or a miner stumbled in with something broken.

But when the door flew open and slammed back against the wall, she knew it wasn't one of those.

Tibby stood in the doorway like something dragged in from the river. His eyes were wild, sunken, skin gone gray beneath the blood and dirt. He had his pistol out, gripped in a shaking hand, pointed more or less at her head.

"I need you," he rasped.

Mattie didn't flinch. Taking a deep, calming breath, she folded the gauze she was working on and set it aside.

"Clearly."

He staggered toward the exam table and dropped onto it, groaning as he pressed a hand to his side. The blood had soaked through two shirts. "Bullet. Left side. Didn't go through."

"I can see that." Mattie walked slowly to the washbasin. "You planning on shooting me before or after I patch you up?"

"Shut up," Tibby growled. His voice was raw, more threat than control. "Just fix me up."

"I'll do that," she said. "But you wave that pistol at me again, I'm going to break your fingers with a hammer before I dig the slug out."

Tibby blinked at her. "You wouldn't dare?"

"Don't bet on it," Mattie said, rolling up her sleeves. "I will not ask who shot you, although I could guess. But I'll take care of you because that's what I do. Now take your coat off. Or die in it. I'm good either way."

Some of his slickness came back. "This isn't how I pictured getting undressed for you."

She snorted. "This is the only way you'll get undressed for me. Ever. Anything else is whiskey-dreams."

Tibby sneered but complied, teeth gritted as he peeled the coat and shirt back, revealing the wound. It was angry and leaking, ringed with burned powder and bruised flesh. The bullet had buried deep, close to his side.

Mattie leaned in, expression unreadable. "You're lucky the bullet missed anything vital. Or unlucky, depending on how this day goes."

She worked in silence, steady and unhurried. The room filled with the scent of alcohol and blood. She sterilized her tools in boiling water, threaded her needle, and began the process with quiet efficiency.

Tibby winced, groaned, cursed. She didn't pause even once.

"Was it Coble that shot you?" she asked casually.

Tibby didn't answer right away. "I thought you weren't going to ask."

She dug deeper with the probe.

He yelped. "Goddamn woman!"

"Sorry," she said, not sounding sorry. "Bullet's lodged against the rib. You move again, and I'll leave it in place. A free piece of advice," she continued, "I think you should leave this country. There's a lot of work in western Kansas, from what I hear. You'd do well there."

Tibby growled. "I'm the law in this town."

"Nah, I don't think so, not anymore." She met his gaze. "At least not with decent folks."

Silence settled again as she worked. Sweat beaded on Tibby's brow. His pistol hand trembled, barely able to keep it raised. She noticed.

"Where's that shiny, new Schofield you had? I'm not sure that beat-up old Colt will fire."

"None of your damned business." Tibby wheezed, grimacing in pain.

"Well, you're bleeding faster than you can bluff. Pretty soon you'll pass out. Then it's my choice what to do with you."

"Fix me first," he muttered.

"That depends. Did you hurt Coble?"

When he didn't answer, she pressed on his wound.

"No." He squirmed on the table. "I don't think any of them were hurt. They shot us to rag dolls."

"Good. I'll fix you up," she said, relieved. "But you better hope I'm in a forgiving mood when I'm done."

Fifteen minutes later, she dropped the bloody slug into a jar with a loud *ping*. Tibby's breathing was ragged. He looked near collapse, face white with shock.

She stitched the wound clean and tight, disinfecting with whiskey, not wanting to use any of the better stuff. Her hands were steady as stone.

When she finished, she stepped back, doused her hands in a washtub up to her elbows, wiped her hands on a rag, and finally looked him in the eye.

"Now," she said, "I don't like you, Tibby. You've got two choices. You walk out that door and leave this town, or you die right here and I feed you to the pigs."

Tibby opened his mouth to speak, but slumped forward instead, half-conscious.

She caught him before he hit the floor, cursed under her breath, and dragged him to the back room, where she kept patients who couldn't walk.

After checking the lock on the clinic door, she grabbed the shotgun from the wall. She stood there a moment, watching Tibby's unconscious form on the cot, and considered all the ways she could make his death look like mercy.

But she didn't pull the trigger.

Not yet.

Maybe Coble would come.

She closed the door to his room, knowing that if he came back through it, she would be warned.

The town of Lamar stirred with the slow rhythm of morning. Boots were clunking on porch steps, roosters crowing in the distance, someone hammering loose shingles back into place—the blacksmith started his incessant beating of iron into submission.

Inside, Mattie sat in her worn chair beside the stove, hands wrapped around a cup of bitter coffee. She hadn't slept, but she wasn't tired, not yet. Her eyes fixed on the back room where she'd left Tibby, stitched, fevered, and breathing like a man who wasn't sure he wanted to live.

The shotgun lay across her lap. Just in case he decided.

She hadn't tied him down. She could've. But she wanted to see what he'd choose. That was the thing about men like Tibby. They always chose wrong eventually.

The clock on the mantel ticked as if daring her to blink.

Mattie's head snapped up.

Too quiet.

She stood, shotgun gripped tight, and moved down the hall.

The cot was empty.

The back window was open.

Blood on the sill.

Outside, the trail of Tibby's escape was crude as a child's drawing. Bloody palm prints, a broken fence rail, the faint scuff of boot heels. He hadn't gotten far, but far enough.

The sharp report of gunfire came from the front of the building.

Mattie stopped. "Dammit, he went for his horse."

When she threw open the front door, Amos was

there, barely standing, one hand pressed to his ribs, his face gone gray under a layer of dust and sweat.

Amos tried to speak, but pitched forward.

Mattie caught him under the arm and eased him down...all she could do with a man his size. "Jesus, Amos. What happened?"

"Tibby. I tried to stop him."

She checked his side. The bullet tore a wide gash along his ribs, leaving more blood than meat. Looking down the alley where Tibby had escaped, her jaw tightened.

This was her fault. In that instant, she understood Coble a lot more. She should have killed Tibby. He would keep killing because she'd missed her opportunity.

Mattie got help from two men walking by, and they hauled Amos into the front room and laid him on the bench. She worked fast, gauze, stitching, boiled water, laudanum in careful doses. It took a lot to sedate a man of his size. Her arms trembled, but not from fear.

Tibby had gotten away.

That would haunt her forever. She knew the deputy would kill again. What if he killed Coble?

Chapter Nineteen

By the time Coble rode into Lamar, the sun hung low and red in the west, staining the streets with shadow. The day had bled itself dry, and the world looked dipped in rust. He rode slow, saddle creaking, hat pulled low against the glare. His horse moved stiff, dust streaking its flanks.

The town sat quiet under the weight of the dying light. Porch rails leaned. A dog lay stretched across the general store stoop, its disinterested gaze too tired to follow the man and his horse. Even the wind sounded weary, but maybe that was just his mood. A few townsfolk peeked from behind curtains or shaded their eyes from porches, but none called out.

Coble could feel it from the saddle...the silence that wasn't peace but aftermath. News had traveled ahead of him.

The fire. The bodies. Tibby.

He passed the telegraph office—closed, the window half-boarded. The sound of his horse's shuffling hooves echoed down the dirt street, a steady cadence.

Mattie's clinic stood at the far end, a single-story building of fading whitewash and determination. The first thing he noticed was footprints and drag marks in blood.

He tied the horse off to the rail and rested a hand against its neck. The animal shivered but didn't pull away. "Easy," he muttered. "We both earned it."

He didn't knock, but opened the door slowly, out of respect.

Inside, the disinfectant smell hit him first. Carbolic, whiskey, and sweat. It clung to the air. Open windows did little to push it out, though lavender hung in bunches to catch the breeze. A tin pot of boiling water and gauze simmered on the stove, and cloth bandages hung from a line strung across the window, fluttering slightly in the heat.

Amos lay on a cot near the wall, half-conscious, with an arm in a sling and his side wrapped tight with linen that had once been white. His breathing came in slow, shallow pulls. Coble had never seen a man's face that pale and still have life in it.

Mattie stood at the washbasin, sleeves rolled past the elbows, her hands red from scrubbing. Her hair had come loose from its knot and hung in stubborn curls around her temples. Lamplight caught the lines at the corners of her eyes, not age, but exhaustion.

She didn't look up when she spoke. "Don't touch anything without washing. I don't want blood on the floor, or dust in my sutures."

Coble removed his hat, brushed the brim once,

and stepped light over the boards. "Didn't mean to track more trouble in."

"You brought it anyway," she said. Then she rinsed her hands, the water turning pink, and finally looked at him. "You heard."

"I heard Tibby came through here."

Mattie's jaw tightened. "Came through, bled on everything, pulled a gun on me, and crawled out my back window like a damn raccoon."

Coble's lips twitched, not in a smile, but something near it. This was a warrior woman, she just didn't realize it. "Did he hurt anyone else?"

"Amos tried to help." Her voice softened, then broke into something brittle. "Got shot for his trouble...again."

Coble's eyes flicked toward the cot. "Which way?"

"I don't know. Some folks said south, but it won't be far. He's too weak. He'll hole up somewhere with shade and bad company."

She grabbed a towel, drying her hands in short, angry motions. Then she met his gaze, her voice suddenly quiet. "You look worse than he does."

"I've been worse," Coble said.

She huffed a small laugh. "That's what worries me."

He stepped closer, lowering his voice. "You holding up, Mattie?"

"I'm breathing. I'll count that as holding." She leaned back against the table, watching him. "How's the ranch?"

"No problems that a hammer and a lot of cussing won't fix. Barn's gone. Shed too. But the house still stands."

"That house sounds like you," she said softly. "Too stubborn to fall down."

He nodded once. "How's Amos for real?"

She sighed. "He's alive because I was right here, lost a lot of blood, though. He's strong as a bull, but not made of iron. I'll send him home tomorrow, let his wife take care of him."

Coble walked to the cot, crouched down beside Amos. The man's chest rose in shallow rhythm, sweat shining on his forehead. Coble laid a hand on the blanket. "You rest easy, old son. You did good."

Mattie's hands paused mid-fold. "He'd follow you to the ranch if you asked."

"It's an open invitation for both of you," Coble said.

She went back to folding linen, voice calmer. "If Amos lives, I'll see if he'll take you up on your offer. He's been shot enough."

Coble raised an eyebrow. "And you?"

"The same argument still applies." She smiled faintly. "I'm a nurse playing doctor, not a deputy, nor a rancher."

"You could do two of those from the ranch," he said.

"I can't chase outlaws, and I can't make that sheriff do more than warm his chair. All I can do is patch people up and pray the one I fixed doesn't kill the man I love."

The words hung there, spoken in truth, anguish, and a bit of surprise at what had blurted out of her mouth.

He looked at her, eyes soft in the lantern light. "We've got a strange way of showing affection."

"Other than...?" she teased, the corner of her mouth lifting.

He smiled, slow and tired. "Other than everything."

They stood for a moment, silence carrying its own warmth. Then she stepped forward, and he met her halfway. The hug was brief but real, the kind that steadies more than it comforts. When she pulled back, her eyes were shining.

"I have to see the sheriff," Coble said.

"Then you're going after Tibby."

"I have to," he replied. "I'm lucky I didn't bury friends because of him. He burned my barn, damn near took my people with it. He won't stop unless someone makes him stop."

Mattie crossed her arms. "I stitched his wound. Deep. He won't heal fast."

"That'll help," Coble said.

Her gaze was steady on his. "You going to kill him?"

"If I can," he said simply.

"Dump it on the sheriff. Make him telegraph for help." Mattie's hands froze over the folded gauze, fear painted her face. "You could walk away."

He gave her a weary smile. "It isn't revenge, Mattie. It's the old saying—if not me, who? If not now, when?"

She nodded slowly. "Then at least do it clean. Don't give him any chances."

Coble reached for his hat. "I don't intend to. There's a special hell that waits for a man like that."

She grabbed something from the counter, a roll of cotton bandage and a tin of salve, and pressed them into his hand. "You'll need these before it's over."

He handed them back. "Got horse liniment. Works the same."

Mattie's eyes softened. "Liniment? You always did mistake pain for progress."

OUTSIDE, the light had gone purple at the edges. The wind had picked up, dragging dust along the boardwalks in little spirals. The whole town seemed to lean west, away from the coming night.

Coble walked slowly to the sheriff's office, boots clicking against old wood. The sign on the door, Sheriff Dennis Springer, burned into a wooden shingle with a hot iron, was faded almost to nothing. In Coble's opinion, like the man.

Inside, lamplight glowed weakly through a dirty globe that hadn't been cleaned since it was new.

Sheriff Springer sat at his desk, polishing a coin with the hem of his shirt. His badge lay unpinned beside it, catching the same faint light. He didn't look up when the door creaked open.

"You're late," he said.

"Late for what?" Coble asked. "You've been expecting me?"

"Late for telling me how I'm not doing my job and that you're going after Tibby. Except"—Springer squinted at the coin—"that's not how this works."

Coble leaned against the doorframe. "Are you going after him?"

"No," Springer said, setting the coin down. "And

you're not either. He's out of my jurisdiction. Hell, he's probably out of the county by now. I admit he's a rotten apple, but there's nothing to be done."

"Funny," Coble said, "I thought the law didn't stop at the edge of a map."

Springer tapped the badge on his desk. "That's why I don't wear it anymore. I just keep it polished in case someone's looking."

Coble's jaw tightened. "Then someone ought to look harder."

The sheriff finally looked up. His face was red and tired, colored by cheap whiskey and worse sleep. "You're not a marshal anymore, Coble. You don't get to go playing hero."

Coble reached into his coat, pulled out the tarnished badge, and pinned it to his vest. The metal caught the lamplight, dull but steady. "I never stopped being one," he said. "The judge didn't want me to advertise it, and I just got sidetracked a bit. As of now, I'm back on paper. When you wire the judge to complain, you can tell him I said you're done. I'll recommend your resignation."

Springer gawked, the sound half a choke. "You can recommend until the cows come home. Won't do you no good. I'm elected by the people."

Coble smiled, thin as a knife. "Watch me."

He turned to leave.

"You go down this trail," Springer called after him, voice rising with desperation, "you're alone. Ain't no cavalry coming. No help."

Coble stopped at the door. "There never was," he said, and stepped into the night.

By the time he rode out again, the moon was climbing over the ridge, sharp and cold. The horse snorted once, restless, but settled when he swung into the saddle. The world was quiet except for the wind in the grass and the sharp cry of a nighthawk.

Riding south along the wagon road that stretched empty ahead, a ribbon of dust silvered by moonlight, he was wary of ambush. He didn't know where Tibby was hiding. But he didn't need to.

He knew how Tibby thought, how a man crawls when he's wounded, how fear makes the mind sharp in the wrong ways. Tibby would pick a place half-ruined, half-forgotten. Somewhere no sheriff would bother to look. Shade, water, maybe a rotten roof. He'd have company, the kind paid in liquor and promises.

Coble rode on, eyes fixed on the horizon. Somewhere out there, the last light of the day gave way to the promise of a reckoning. He could almost smell the smoke from the burned barn, hear the hiss of a lantern burning bright.

He adjusted the rifle beneath his leg, the metal cool against his thigh. The stars came out full and bright enough to cut.

The horse stumbled once on the rutted trail and then found its rhythm again. Coble leaned forward, murmuring softly, "We're almost there, boy. Just a little farther. Rats always come home to their nests."

The night wind carried his words off into the distance.

And in that wind, faint and low, came another sound, the echo of hoofbeats not his own.

He didn't look back. Not yet.

He just smiled, slow and grim.

"Found you," he whispered.

Then he kicked the horse into a gallop and rode into the dark.

Chapter Twenty

WITH COBLE GONE ON TIBBY'S TRAIL, THE RANCH settled into a rhythm that was quiet but not idle. The days passed hot and long, each hour filled with hammer blows, sawdust, and the scent of scorched pine.

The barn was gone. Burned to its stone foundation. The shed too. But the house still stood—battered, blackened in places, but upright.

War Eagle and String Bean took it personally.

They rebuilt not like cowhands patching something up, but like soldiers digging in. Every board they nailed down, every fencepost driven deep, meant the ranch stood strong.

War Eagle stood shirtless on the porch roof, hammer in one hand, sweat cutting through the dust on his chest. Below him, String Bean was sawing a length of board with a rhythm that sounded almost like music.

"We oughta build a lookout tower," String Bean said.

"For what?" War Eagle grunted.

"Snipers. Outlaws. Ghosts. You know. Thursday stuff."

"We ain't building no tower. We finish the porch, we reinforce the door frame, and we make sure that the second-floor hallway's a bottleneck. And then we fix the firing ports in the upstairs shutters. That's defense."

"Fine," String Bean muttered. "But I'm calling dibs on the shotgun if ghosts show up."

"Why ghosts?"

"With all the bones coming out of that creek out there? You kidding me?"

War Eagle paused, then chuckled. "Fair."

They worked like that, one always teasing, one always practical. The banter kept their hands moving when their minds wanted to wander to distant crossroads and wanted men who bent the law to suit themselves. The work itself was a comfort, it punished quiet worry with the honest ache of labor. Each battered board replaced was an argument made and won against fear.

INSIDE, Adelina moved through the house like a whirling dervish, with eyes that caught everything and gave away nothing. War Eagle had told her she was like iron, the harder she pushed, the stronger she got. She took pride in that.

After the fire, she'd taken charge of inside the house, cleaned soot from the walls, helped replace broken windows, soaked linens in vinegar and lye until they no longer smelled of smoke. She cooked with quiet purpose, and anyone who tried to help her usually got a ladle in the chest and a pointed glare. But she made time to bring cold water to the porch crew, and her hands lingered a little longer each day when she passed War Eagle the jug.

They didn't want for food, and she kept it ready. She kept a tin of coffee on the stove and made it last. The scent of frying potatoes, chicken, and coffee took the place of char and soot. It filled the house and overrode the smell of sawdust and hot metal from the smithing of repairs.

The kitchen table, worn smooth from years of use, became their council. There, they set plans: which fence to put up, which cattle would stay and which should be driven to safer ground.

That evening, the three of them sat at the kitchen table, too tired to talk much.

Adelina poured coffee, stiff and black. War Eagle watched her hands, strong and elegant. She had scars on two fingers, old burns.

She noticed his gaze. "From a boiling pot," she said simply. "When I was fifteen. Burned bad. But I finished the meal."

"You cook for a living or a fight?" he asked.

"For both. My mother died early. My father was a constable in Fort Scott. He kept all hours, so things had to be ready."

He grinned. "Are you always this bossy?"

"Are you always this slow?" She sipped her coffee, glancing at him over the top.

String Bean snorted into his cup. "Can I leave the table, or should I pretend I'm invisible?"

Adelina stood. "You could go feed the chickens. They'll come to roost if you put feed inside the pen."

"They hate me," String Bean groused.

"They can tell you're afraid of them." She laughed. "Bluff them out. Their eyes are bigger than their brains."

String Bean dragged himself outside, muttering.

The silence after he left was long and companionable.

War Eagle looked down at his cup, turning it slowly in his hand. "You stayed with us after the fire. Most women would have left."

Adelina shrugged. "I had my reasons."

He glanced at her. "That so?"

She wiped her hands on a towel and leaned against the counter. "You know what I learned while working in the city? Men leave. Even the good ones. Especially the good ones. I just never had the time to sort them out."

She paused for a moment, looking around. "But this house...this place. It feels different. Like something's trying to take root here."

He nodded slowly. "I feel that too."

"Then you need to be patient. With me."

War Eagle nodded, trying not to show his disappointment. "I can do that."

She crossed her arms. "You think Coble's coming back?"

"If he doesn't," War Eagle said, "I'll go find him. Drag him back by his boot heels."

"And if Tibby comes first?"

"I don't think he will. It cost him too much the last

time. But no matter, we still have to be ready, for him or anyone else."

Her eyes flicked to the rifle leaning against the wall.

He followed her gaze. "You know how to use one?"

Adelina stepped forward, picked up the rifle, and worked the action smooth as butter. She checked the chamber, satisfied, then looked him dead in the eye. "I've buried my father here, and he was a good man. Being a police officer, he also taught me how to use firearms. This was one of my favorites."

War Eagle smiled. "I believe you."

She looked at him a moment longer than necessary. Then, she set the rifle down and moved past him, close enough for him to feel the heat off her shoulder.

Before she left the room, she paused. "You missed a nail on the east wall. That board will work loose if you don't fix it."

He grinned. "You sure you don't want to marry me?"

She looked back, expression unreadable. "Ask me when you're finished building something that lasts, when our future looks a little more stable."

Then she was gone, carrying a mop and pail upstairs.

He stared after her. It might take years to accomplish that.

OUTSIDE, String Bean called from the yard, "Damned chickens are conspiring again."

War Eagle stood, coffee forgotten.

He looked around the kitchen. Anytime he entered, he couldn't help but feel hungry. The smell of fried chicken still lingered. And the biscuits and gravy? God, they were going to be fat if they weren't careful. He sighed, his mind on what Adelina had said. *We have something worth bleeding for. Right here in this place.*

Then he went out to save String Bean from conspiring chickens.

THE DAYS that followed blurred into a slow, stubborn succession of tasks. String Bean proved better at tall tales than at carpentry. Half the time his boards lay crooked, and half the time they were exactly right because he'd improvised a fix that made the thing stronger. He told a story about his uncle building a roof in a gale wind and how the roof had held the whole town in one piece, the men laughed and hammered and nailed it true.

War Eagle, for his part, kept watch. The idea of a tower had been tossed aside in favor of practical measures, but he took to staying up later than the others, patrolling the perimeter at dusk when the bugs rose in clouds and the heat finally surrendered. He walked the fence lines with the rifle slung over his shoulder, checking for disturbed soil, for footprints that weren't cattle. Once he found a set, not fresh, but a day old, that led off toward the KATY tracks. He made a note of it and then walked the line again until the night made him feel safer.

Sometimes he thought of Coble, the way he hunted, methodical and quiet, the narrow set of his jaw when he read a trail. Coble's absence left a hollow where certainty had been. There were other hollows. The smell of the burned timbers, the way the horses kept a sliver of unease in their eyes. But the men filled the hollows with work, and Adelina filled them with food and order.

On a day when the sky hung low and the heat pressed against the land like an accusation, War Eagle rigged up a half-circle of sandbags at the northern window. He filled them with the black loam from the garden.

String Bean bristled at the ugliness. "It looks like a fort," he said, and Adelina said nothing, only arranged a small shelf of jugs near the window so they'd have water if they hunkered down.

Neighbors came and went. A lean man from a neighboring farm saw they were building and asked to borrow a plank. War Eagle gave him two, and the man left with a look that said he didn't know how to be thankful. A couple from the southern road brought eggs and news. Someone claimed to have seen Tibby in a saloon south of Lamar. War Eagle made no promises, the man left in a hurry. Rumors were like flies, they landed where you fed them and left a sticky mess.

At night, the house hummed with a guarded sleep. They took turns at the window, but it was less about fear than about duty. War Eagle would wake in the small hours, look out where the sky met the horizon, and imagine the figures he'd forced into his memory. Mattie with her clinic, Coble with his stubborn devotion, Tibby with that quick, cruel grin. He would watch the stars, listen to the distant sound of the

KATY locomotive like a groaning beast far away, and sometimes allow himself a small bitterness toward the rail that had brought strangers and trouble through their patch of earth.

There were small mercies. A foal was born one morning, legs wobbling, ears damp. Adelina had insisted the mare deserved a clean stall and a bucket of oats. The baby's first breath and first whinny felt like a promise. War Eagle stood in the dawn and watched it wobble toward life, and for a moment, his hands forgot the weight of hammer and gun both.

String Bean found an old tin harmonica in a desk drawer and taught himself a tune. It was a clumsy, cheerful thing that seemed to loosen the air. Once, while they ate under the porch overhang, Adelina hummed along and String Bean played a little, and War Eagle felt the edges of his world soften. Laughter came easier after that, and even the cattle seemed to settle.

But there were harder lessons. They practiced maneuvers in the yard: how to move silently between stacks of wood, how to keep to shadows, how to put a wedge under the kitchen door so it would hold for more than a minute. War Eagle showed them how to make a makeshift tripline and where to set it to give warning without killing a man. Deterrence then, not execution. He did not like killing, never had, even when forced. But he practiced on targets. He'd heard the saying, *speed is fine, but accuracy is everything*. He believed it.

One dusk, as the sun fell beneath a wash of purple, War Eagle and Adelina sat on the newly repaired porch steps. The work had made them quieter companions, settled, more honest. The conversation flowed like the soft water in a creek...not deep, but enough to keep things moving.

"You were young once," she said, watching his hands. "I bet you laughed every day, before the things you've held onto weighed you down."

He gave a small, wry grin. "I was young and have been foolish occasionally."

"You've been a good man for this place," she said. "That matters."

"It's not just me," he answered. "It's what's here. You, mostly. And String Bean. It's the smell of the prairie at dusk, the wind across the tall grass. I've come to love it here. The place and the company. All the things that feel like home."

She turned her face toward him. For a heartbeat, there was an openness in her, a door left slightly ajar. Then she closed it and said, "You're a good man, Mr. Parker."

War Eagle nodded, and she didn't need to say more. A commitment was not always a ring or a vow, sometimes it was a willingness to bear a night watch, to bake bread in scarcity, to keep a rifle clean and loaded for a man who might never return.

Night fell, and crickets took up the job the men had left unfinished. The house settled under the sky's wide, indifferent gaze. On the table, a candle guttered, throwing a small pool of light across the plans for the next week. A new fence line, a cistern to catch more rain, reinforcement across the back door. They would do it all. They had already begun.

Before turning in, War Eagle walked the perimeter one last time. The moon left a silver path along

Runaway Creek. The footprints were there again, faint in the packed dirt by the ditch. He kneeled and brushed his fingers through the soil as if it might tell him more than supposition and day-old shoe impressions. He listened for the night sounds. The coyotes barked like old dogs, an owl's lonely cry, and he felt the old, stubborn fierceness in his chest.

If Coble didn't come back soon, War Eagle would go find him. If Tibby came instead, they'd be ready. The thought settled in him, practical, irrevocable.

He shouldered his rifle, tasted the dust on his lips, thinking of the cool water from the well, and walked back toward the warm light of the house where Adelina was sure to be stirring bread or coffee. He smiled...or trouble. The ranch had been put to the test. Walls had bent, but the center held. They would rebuild it stronger, and if need be, they would bleed to keep it so.

Inside, String Bean was snoring softly on a pallet in front of the stove, the harmonica within reach. Adelina had gone upstairs to her room, leaving the mop propped in the corner like a silent sentinel. War Eagle stood in the doorway a moment longer before moving to a last cup of coffee before he turned in.

Outside, the stars watched the ranch like small, indifferent sentinels. War Eagle closed the door quietly behind him and sat in the rocker on the porch. It had been a good week. They were ready.

Chapter Twenty-One

Coble rode west through the long morning heat. Every mile back toward Lamar felt heavier, as if the land itself were watching, waiting for the next wound. The KATY tracks ran beside him for a while, rails humming faintly under the sun, the distant whistle of a locomotive drifting downwind in ghostly sound. He was sure of it, someone would write about that sound someday.

He'd lost Tibby again. That thought gnawed at him worse than thirst. Coble had seen plenty of men vanish before, some into bad weather, some into bad luck. But Tibby carried something darker. A sickness that festered in his soul and spread to anyone who stood too close.

The horse's stride slowed, and Coble eased up on the reins. "Easy, boy," he murmured. The dun's sides shone with sweat, and every breath came hard. They both needed water and rest. He found a narrow draw with a trickle of creek running through it, dismounted, and crouched to fill his hat with cool water. When he splashed it over his face, the world came back sharp and clean.

The reflection that stared back from the creek was of a man carved down to purpose, no law badge, no mercy, just the line of a jaw and a set of eyes that had seen too many graves.

He thought of the ranch, of War Eagle and String Bean rebuilding the porch, of Adelina's hands cleaning soot from the walls. He could almost smell her coffee.

They earned their place at the ranch, while he rode in circles chasing a ghost.

By the time he reached the outskirts of Lamar, evening shadows stretched long, and the air carried the heavy scent of smoke from cook fires. He rode straight to Mattie's clinic. One horse graced the hitch rail, and she'd propped open the door to let in what little breeze there was.

Inside, the place smelled of soap, the bitter tang of medicine fighting to cover the scent of blood and sweat. Mattie stood over a patient, her sleeves rolled to the elbows, hair tied back tight. She didn't look up when he stepped inside.

"You're tracking dirt through my floor again," she said.

Coble glanced at his boots. "I brought it with good intentions."

"That'll be the first time dirt's ever done that."

He waited until she tied off the bandage and stepped aside.

A bowlegged man with an arm wound tipped his

hat to Mattie. "Thank you, Miss Mattie. The boss will be in to settle up for your work. Maybe do some trading? Cash money is hard to come by right now."

"Whatever you think is fair, Hiram." Mattie smiled at the man.

He gave Coble a curious look on his way out.

They watched the man mount and ride away.

"I missed him again, Mattie. Tibby is slippery as a greased pig."

She looked at him then, eyes sharp as scalpels. "And?"

"He's hurt, still bleeding. But it's not slowing him down."

Her hands froze on the cloth she was folding. For a moment, she said nothing. "You had him, didn't you?"

"I had him."

"And?"

Coble shook his head. "He ran. We traded shots."

Mattie turned away, setting the folded cloth down a little too hard. "You'll chase him again."

"Yes."

"You'll keep chasing him until one of you's in the ground."

He didn't answer. Some truths didn't need air.

She exhaled through her nose, then softened. "You're not the same, Coble. You used to chase men for justice. Now it feels like you just revel in the chase."

He looked toward the window, where the light had gone gold with dusk. "Maybe there's no difference anymore."

Mattie moved closer, lowering her voice. "You will not find peace this way."

"Peace ain't on this trail, Mattie."

"No," she whispered. "And it's not waiting at the end of a gun, either."

Coble put his hat back on. "He's south of here. I figure he'll look for me at the ranch."

Mattie caught his wrist as he turned to go. "If you find him, make it quick. Don't give him a chance."

Coble's gaze flicked to her hand, then to her face. "I don't plan to." He paused. "Mattie?" he continued, "come with me. Let me take you to the ranch."

"We've been through this, Coble. My place is here."

When he left, she let him go. The door shut behind him with a soft thud, and the night took him again. If there were a place for the two of them, she hoped they'd find it soon.

THE EVENING SETTLED heavy and still at the ranch on Runaway Creek. The smell of pine and sawdust hung in the air. War Eagle and String Bean sat on the porch steps, the new boards creaking beneath them, the sound of crickets filling the dark.

Adelina came out with a lantern, setting it on the railing between them. Its glow painted their faces amber.

"No word?" she asked.

War Eagle shook his head. "Not yet."

String Bean spat into the dirt. "He'll bring Tibby back, or he won't come back at all."

Adelina shot him a sharp look. "Don't talk like that."

"I'm just saying what we're all thinking."

War Eagle's gaze stayed on the dark horizon. "Coble's too mean to die easy. He'll show up."

Adelina folded her arms. "Sometimes that's not enough."

They fell into silence again, each listening to the quiet in their own way. The night seemed to stretch wider, the shadows deeper. Somewhere out past the barn, a coyote yipped and was answered by another farther off. Probably all coming for water at Runaway Creek.

After a while, String Bean stood. "I'll check that fence line tomorrow."

War Eagle nodded, but his eyes didn't leave the road.

Adelina lingered beside him. "Do you think he'll catch him this time?"

"He will," War Eagle said. "But catching a man like Tibby doesn't always mean bringing him home."

She studied his face in the lantern light. "You think Coble's still chasing Tibby...or something inside himself?"

"Maybe both."

Adelina's gaze drifted toward the stars, faint in the thin blue dark. "Sometimes I think all of you men are chasing something you'll never find."

War Eagle smiled faintly, watching her. "Sometimes we find it right in front of us."

Far off, down the road that ran along the tracks, a shape formed, a rider moving slow, hat low, dust trailing like a ghost's veil.

Adelina's breath caught. "Is that?"

"I see him."

They watched in silence as the horse plodded closer until the rider came into the lantern's reach. Coble's face looked carved from stone. Dust coated his shoulders, and his eyes were darker than the night behind him.

He swung down from the saddle without a word.

"Where's Tibby?" War Eagle asked.

Coble sighed, shook his head. "Gone."

"Dead?"

"No. Just gone."

The single word hung heavy. Gone.

Adelina's expression softened, but she said nothing. She could see the way his shoulders sagged, how his hands shook just a little as he unbuckled his gun belt and laid it across the porch rail.

War Eagle studied him. "You hurt?"

"Only my pride." He sighed. "And my belly thinks my throat's been cut."

"Then sit at the table," Adelina said, already turning toward the kitchen. "I'll serve up a meal."

Coble nodded once and sank down onto the step. String Bean appeared out of the dark, grin half-hidden. "Chickens are roosting, boss. Nobody shot at us. It's a good day."

"Let's keep it that way," Coble said.

Adelina returned a few minutes later with coffee and bread, and the simple mercy of a hot meal. She handed him the cup, and for a while no one spoke. The sound of the wind through the grass filled the silence between them.

Finally, Coble said, "He's south of Lamar, east of here. I can't say where. He's hurt, but he's holed up. I figure he's found shelter. He was at the old mill near the ridge, but I didn't find him."

War Eagle nodded slowly. "Then we'll be ready if he turns back."

Coble looked up at the night. The stars seemed colder than he remembered. "He will," he said quietly. "Men like Tibby always circle back to what they tried to burn."

Adelina set a hand on War Eagle's shoulder, steady and sure. "Then we'll meet him here."

Coble looked at her hand—calloused, strong, a working hand—and then at the house behind her. The porch boards were new, but the foundation still carried the scent of smoke. They were all rebuilding something, even if none of them knew exactly what.

He tipped his hat slightly. "Reckon I'll take the first watch."

War Eagle stood. "I reckon you won't. You're not alone in this, and you're all used up. You rest up tonight. When you leave tomorrow, you'll have a good meal in you."

Coble looked doubtful. "But a man's got to earn the right to rest."

"You already have," String Bean said. "Take a walk, settle yourself, and then get some sleep. We'll stand guard."

Adelina watched Coble walk out into the yard, the lantern glow fading against his back. He stopped by the fence, looking out over the dark prairie where the wind whispered through the grass like the voice of some patient, watching god.

Behind him, the ranch creaked softly, alive, breathing, waiting. The chicken coop rustled and clucked.

Horses in the pen stomped, tails switching, some leaning against the fence rails to test their strength. And JoeBoy, their new resident jackass, walked sentry duty around the coop waiting for any luckless coyote or fox trying for a chicken meal.

Coble rested a hand on the fence rail and let his eyes follow the northern ridge. Somewhere beyond it, a wounded man was under the same moon, bleeding and desperate.

It would end soon. One way or another.

And when it did, maybe this land would finally be quiet again.

Chapter Twenty-Two

CROSSROADS WERE ALWAYS BAD PLACES FOR COBLE.

Too many choices. Too many ways for a man to vanish.

Jubal's Crossing was no different. It was a stretch of dusty trail flanked by the KATY Railroad on one side and a half-rotten knot of buildings on the other—a saloon, a livery stable, a general store with a faded sign, and a hotel that hadn't seen clean sheets since Grant was president. The hotel's porch sagged in the middle like a swayback mule, and a single lantern swung from a bent nail, its flame guttering against the rising dusk.

Coble reined in at the edge of town. His horse, a rangy dun, blew hard and stamped at the ground, nostrils flaring. The air smelled of rotgut whiskey and clothes seldom washed.

He studied the saloon. Or meeting hall. It didn't have a name. Judging from the number of horses tied to the hitch rail, business was good. A few had bedrolls lashed behind their saddles—drovers, cowhands, or men passing through. Others carried no such burden, their tack too clean, their rigs too fine. Locals...men for hire. And one roan gelding, dusty, restless, pawing the ground. Coble's jaw tightened. Still warm. Still sweaty.

Tibby was inside.

Coble dismounted, letting his hand trail down the gelding's neck. The hide was slick with sweat, the hair clumped from a long ride. He took a breath, slid his hat low against the dying light, and checked his pistols.

Both Schofield's rode easy in his holsters, hammers unlooped. Men who forgot that simple precaution tended to die with their guns still strapped. He thumbed open one cylinder—full. Always full. He rolled his shoulders once, feeling the grit of the road trickle down his back, then stepped up onto the warped boardwalk. The boards creaked under his boots, one plank giving slightly where a knot had rotted through. The saloon door groaned open, releasing a gust of heat.

Inside was the usual mix of cheap whiskey, old sweat, and trouble. Smoke hung low like a haze that never quite left. The piano in the corner rattled out a sour waltz, the tune a man played when he'd forgotten all others but couldn't stop his hands from moving. A card game murmured near the back. Glasses clinked. The laughter of men who didn't care who was watching filled the gaps.

Coble's eyes adjusted. The room was darker than the outside glare, and shadows paid rent in every corner. He scanned once, noting the door, window, bar, piano, a bar stool dandy leading a painted lady up the stairs to a communal room, and then he saw him.

Tibby.

Sitting near the back wall at a round table, a bottle half-drained in front of him. Two men flanked him, hard-eyed and greasy, the company a man hired when he didn't expect to live long. Tibby looked thinner than Coble remembered, but there was a coiled tightness in him still, a mean, restless animal twitch around the eyes. His left arm rested gingerly against his side, a wound still fresh.

Their eyes met across the room. No one else noticed their interaction. No one else cared.

Coble didn't speak. He didn't even hesitate. His hand moved on instinct, down, across, drawing the Schofield from his belly holster in one clean motion. The gun came free with a sibilant hiss of leather, and the hammer cocked back with a sound as sharp as breaking ice.

Nothing quiets a room faster than the hammer being drawn back on a revolver.

The bottle in front of Tibby exploded before he could lift it. He was up in an instant, table flipping, chair skittering backward. The two men at his sides scrambled, one reaching for his gun, the other half-ducking as if that might save him, and then dove headfirst through the closed window, taking the frame with him.

Tibby's first shot punched into the wall just behind Coble's shoulder. The second shattered a lantern on the bar, spraying glass and flaming kerosene across the wall in a shower of light.

Then hell broke loose.

The saloon turned into a box of thunder. Drunks scattered like startled birds. One man dove awkwardly through the open doorway. Another took cover behind the bar, shouting curses that disappeared in the gunfire. The piano lid slammed shut with a melodious bang.

Coble dove to the left, rolling behind an upturned table. The edge splintered as a bullet ripped through it. He came up in a crouch, sights already lined. His first shot found the man on Tibby's left, as he stepped in front of Tibby, spinning him backward with a wet grunt. The second bullet hit the wall just above Tibby's head, close enough to make him duck.

Tibby fired back, two shots, wild and fast. One clipped Coble's hat, the other shattered a bottle on the back shelf, raining liquor down like rain. The fire, already started with the shattered lamp, spread quickly through the whiskey. The room took on an orange glow, like a sunset over a forest fire.

Smoke stung Coble's eyes. He moved low and steady, using the chaos like a curtain. "You're running out of places to hide, Tibby," he called out, his voice flat, almost calm.

"Still got more than you," came the reply from somewhere behind the rising smoke. "I've been fixing hideouts for years."

Another shot, too high. Coble ducked, swept his revolver along the shadows. The firelight licked the walls, dancing shapes like devils. For a moment, he caught sight of Tibby's silhouette, hat gone, eyes wild, guns in both hands now. Then he was gone again.

The next sound wasn't a gunshot but a creak, the slow, traitorous whine of the back door hinges.

Coble lunged forward, kicking through the smoke. The door banged once against the wall, then swung half-shut again. He burst through into the alley.

Empty. How the hell did he get away so fast?

Just a narrow cut between buildings, choked with garbage and dust. The smell of piss and smoke. His boots struck dirt and slipped on something else, blood, maybe. He looked left. Nothing. Right, the gate was open.

He ran.

The sound of his boots echoed against the walls. The air out here was cooler, but it burned his throat all the same. When he cleared the gate, the last of the sun had dropped behind the hills, and the world turned to twilight and dust.

Then he heard it. Hoofbeats pounding away.

Coble turned toward the sound, and there he was. Tibby was already twenty yards down the road, bent low in the saddle, the roan gelding throwing dirt behind it like a smoke screen. He was heading north, back toward Lamar. Toward home.

Coble raised his pistol, sighting along the barrel. The Schofield felt heavy, patient. He drew a slow breath, steadied...fired.

The shot cracked the dusk wide open. Dust puffed beyond Tibby's horse, a clear miss, and the outlaw never slowed. The sound of hooves faded, swallowed by the open land.

Coble stood there, revolver still raised, smoke curling up from the barrel. He could fire again. He could empty the cylinder, chase the echo of a bullet across the prairie. But he didn't. He'd probably miss the bobbing target anyway. Hitting anything beyond fifty yards with a pistol was either luck or a lie.

He holstered the gun and let the silence settle. The weight of failure came down on him like the grit of the road, light enough to ignore, heavy enough to stay. Damn a man who wouldn't stand and fight.

Behind him, the saloon belched flame through its front windows. A few men stumbled out, coughing, dragging another between them. The bartender's voice rose above the noise, half fury, half fear. "You gonna pay for all this damage, Marshal?"

Coble turned, smoke curling around him. He glanced through the window. The wall was scorched black, the piano smoldering, chairs and tables broken like ribs. People beat at the flames with wet blankets and water buckets. The bartender glared at him from behind what was left of the bar, eyes red and wet.

"Send the bill to Dennis Springer in Lamar," Coble said. "The sheriff will take care of you."

He walked to his horse, mounted up, and looked north. The sky was bruised purple, stars just beginning to wake. He should've turned west, back toward the ranch, back to the people who might still believe in him. Instead, he touched his heels to the horses' sides and followed the road north, toward the dark line of the horizon, where the sound of Tibby's flight had already vanished.

Not home.

Not yet.

THE NIGHT DEEPENED FAST. A wind came up from the east, stirring dust across the trail. The moon was a thin cut of silver over the prairie. Coble rode without hurry but without rest. His thoughts moved like the horse, steady, deliberate, haunted by rhythm.

He thought of Mattie and her clinic in Lamar, how Tibby had held her at gunpoint not days ago, forcing her to stitch him up. The outlaw deputy had nerve... and cruelty. The man might be a lot of things, but he was no coward. Coble's jaw clenched hard enough to ache. He'd seen men like Tibby all his life, the ones who couldn't stand being small, so they tried to make others smaller.

But there was something worse in Tibby now, something new. The fire at the ranch had changed him. Wounded him, yes, but also freed him from whatever decency he'd once faked.

The trail curved along the railroad for a stretch. Coble looked out over the prairie, where the grass rippled under moonlight, silver on black. It reminded him how big the world was, and how small a man could be inside it.

He stopped at a creek a few miles north, let the horse drink, and crouched by the water, upstream from the horse. He'd once been a man who followed the law like it was gospel. Now he was chasing vengeance, or duty, or something meaner that he couldn't quite name.

The night stretched on. Somewhere out there, Coble imagined Tibby was nursing his wound and thinking himself clever. He'd find another town, another dark corner to hide in. But the frontier had a way of shrinking for men like that. You could ride for miles, hide behind rivers and ridges, but the land always remembered your name.

BY DAWN, Coble reached an old rail siding. The station was long abandoned, nothing but a shack and a rusted water tower leaning slightly east. He dismounted, stretched his back, and looked for tracks.

There, hoofprints in the dirt, one set deeper than the rest, fresh. The roan's gait was uneven. Tibby's wound was slowing him, his horse was tired. The tracks led toward a ridge beyond the rail spur line, where cottonwoods marked the line of a creek bed.

Coble squatted by the prints, running a finger through the disturbed earth. The edges were crisp. He wasn't far behind.

He mounted again and nudged his horse forward. The sun was climbing now, hot and merciless. Sweat pooled under his hatband. The land stretched wide and empty, with no sound but the creak of saddle leather and the steady rhythm of hooves.

He crested the ridge and stopped short.

Below, a scatter of rocks, a low fire pit, smoke still rising. A few embers winked in the morning light. He scanned the area. No horse, no rider. But the ashes were warm. Tibby had been here not an hour ago.

Coble dismounted, kicked through the coals. Found a bloodied bandage, crusted dry. Tibby's handiwork. He'd patched himself again. Sloppy work. Desperate work.

He stood there for a long moment, hat in his hand, listening. The breeze carried nothing but heat and the sound of cicadas. He could follow the trail again, could ride until his horse dropped and still be a step too late.

He holstered his pistol, which had appeared unbidden in his hand, turned to the north, and squinted into the light.

"Keep running," he muttered. "See where it gets you."

Then he mounted up, turning the horse west, not toward rest, not toward peace, but toward the long shadow of unfinished business. Tibby was out there, alive and angry. But for the first time, Coble realized something else: he wasn't chasing a man anymore. He was chasing what the fire had taken from them all, justice, or maybe redemption. Maybe there wasn't a difference.

He felt stupid. It made no sense to chase Tibby at this point. Tibby would come to him. And after that, he'd go for Mattie. That was Coble's soft spot. He would not, could not, let anything happen to Mattie. It was time to go home.

Behind him, the wind whispered through the tall grass. Ahead, the horizon waited.

And somewhere between the two, a man like Tibby would have to make his final choice.

Coble adjusted his hat, set his jaw, and rode on.

Chapter Twenty-Three

TIBBY FOOLED HIM.

It wasn't any great trick, no sleight of hand or elaborate deception, just the blunt, desperate cunning that men learn when they've got nothing left to lose. While Coble watched the dark and well-traveled trails, Tibby rode to Lamar by a crooked road Coble never thought to check.

Mattie's clinic sat on the town's main street, windows curtained against the late afternoon heat. She had been cleaning up after late cases, a boy with a sprained wrist, a woman with a cough. And then the bell over the door jangled, and a stranger stepped in. He was clean-shaven and apologetic. He asked if he could talk to her. Mattie, who had tended harder men and kinder ones both, pointed him to a chair. She figured he had a painfully embarrassing problem he might have picked up next door, although she doctored the painted ladies regularly. Since she was almost old enough to be the boy's mother, he might confide in her.

Tibby came in behind him.

She should have seen him. Maybe she did at first and misread the shape of the man who followed. Maybe she thought of him like every other traveler who'd walked into the clinic needing kindness. You can only be wary for so long before it hardens into suspicion and then to a dull, heavy exhaustion.

Tibby closed the door soft as a secret, turned, and shot the young man sitting in the chair. The man would carry his surprised expression to the grave along with a hole in his heart.

Mattie flinched and then dropped the clutch of bandages she was holding, stunned and then anguished as she watched the light go out in the young man's eyes.

"You're fast with your hands," Tibby said, smiling through powder-smoke, an ugly split of a smile that reached for gentleness and found only cruelty. The gun he held on her was steady. "Now you reach into that pocket of yours and take out that pistol you're so handy with. Lay it on that counter over there."

Mattie moved toward the medicine cabinet, feeling the small muscle of her jaw tighten. "Why are you here, Tibby? The way you skulked out of here the last time, I thought you took my advice. What are you doing?"

He shrugged, taking off his hat. The room smelled of disinfectant and hot metal and the faint thread of smoke. Tibby's eyes were small and bright as knife points. "I don't aim to hurt you," he said. "That is... unless you like that sort of thing."

"You ought to leave, Tibby," Mattie said. "You come in here, and you make trouble you can't possibly handle. The sheriff has someone who actually does rounds now. They'll have heard that shot."

"Against the noise of the saloon next door? I don't think so. Besides, laws don't stretch much farther than men care to walk, and his new men are lazy," he answered. "No one is coming by to save you."

Her hand was over her pounding heart. She was still close to her pistol, waiting for a distraction. "I wasn't aware I needed saving."

"Well, maybe just a little," he said. "I sent a rider with a note to Coble. I expect he'll be here sometime tonight."

"Are you that anxious to die?" she asked.

He laughed softly. "That's not what will happen."

Tibby stepped closer, pistol steady on her chest. "You stitch up things that other people think aren't worth sewing together, like me. That's respectable, Doc. That's proper. I want people to see how proper you are."

It was not a joke. What she'd suspected came full bore like a punch in the gut. Tibby was crazy, and there was no telling what he would do.

Mattie moved for the pistol, but his hand was faster. He caught her wrist with the grip of a man who had practiced such moves before. She tasted copper at the back of her throat, blood, maybe, or the fear that makes the mouth dry and metallic.

"You want something," she said, voice steady though her muscles trembled. "Say it."

"What I want is simple." He tightened once, and she felt the breath leave her. "I want you, but you have to come willingly. I know you want me, most women do. But you'll have to lure Coble in first, so I can kill him."

Her laugh was a small, sharp sound that might have been brave or might have been terrified. "That all? I want no part of you."

When Tibby slapped her, she bounced off the counter and landed on her hands and knees. Before she could move, he kicked her, his boot hooking her stomach and lifting her off the floor.

Leaning over her, he said, "I'm pretty sure you'll change your mind."

She gave him a bloody smile. "It doesn't matter what I do. You're a dead man. Why don't you save us all the trouble and kill yourself?"

This time, his boot took her in the ribs.

"Maybe this is a better plan after all. I meant for him to come and find you...after I'm done with you. I had planned to be long gone. But I think I'll just wait until he walks in the door. I want to see his face up close when I kill him. Then I'll finish with you."

She knew Coble would come. And when he did, Tibby would be waiting with whatever fury and cruelty he could muster, and he had both in abundance.

Mattie was not that fragile, she had a spine that didn't like being bent. She measured her options in the seconds between moves—smash the lamp and blind him, throw herself at the door and run, scream and bring every passing stranger into it. None of those seemed like they'd work. Play for time.

She bit her lip and feathered her voice into something like obedience.

"Do what you want. You will anyway."

Tibby smiled like a man given a gift. "Good girl."

Chapter Twenty-Four

The stars were cold when Coble reached the edge of the ravine.

Below him stretched the skeleton of an old sawmill—just a roof and rusted bones left to rot beside a dry creek bed. The wind whistled through the broken slats, carrying the creak of metal and the damp smell of mold.

He reined in the horse and waited, listening.

The night was quiet in that dangerous way, where sound carries too far, and silence seems to mean something was holding its breath. His eyes swept the shadows, tracing every jagged outline, the water tower that leaned like a drunk, the half-buried wagon axle catching moonlight, the glint of glass from a shattered bottle near the door.

It looked like the place a man might crawl into when he was half-dead and mean enough to keep breathing.

Tibby's kind of place.

Coble dismounted, looping the reins over a

mesquite branch. His boots sank into the soft dirt as he walked down the slope. The air smelled faintly of kerosene and rot—the signature of men who didn't stay anywhere long enough to clean it.

At the mill's doorway, he paused, hand brushing the butt of his pistol. The Schofield hung light and familiar at his side, its weight both comfort and curse.

He eased forward, his shoulder brushing the wall. The inside was black as pitch, but for a slit of moonlight through a hole in the roof. Dust drifted like ash. In the corner, a small fire had lingered, leaving a few glowing embers that pulsed faintly, like the last beats of a dying heart.

Coble crouched beside it, running his fingers through the ashes. Warm. Not more than a few hours.

He straightened, scanning again. There were boot prints in the dirt, three pairs at least. One set smaller, uneven. Tibby's maybe favoring his left leg.

He followed them to a rough pallet of hay and cloth, where blood stained the edge. A torn shirt lay nearby, stiff with dried sweat. He picked it up and sniffed. Whiskey and wound rot.

Coble's mouth tightened. "You're bleeding out somewhere close," he murmured.

Behind him, the wind shifted. A coyote barked from the ridge.

When he turned back toward his horse, he saw the flicker of a campfire far off to the east. It was too bright, too steady for a traveler's fire. A signal, maybe. Or bait.

He didn't move toward it. Not yet. He made a cold camp half a mile downwind in a dry wash. Chewing tough jerky, he drank from his canteen, every swallow tasting of metal.

When he finally stretched out on his blanket, he didn't close his eyes. He lay there, hat pulled low, listening to the wind move across the land.

His mind turned to Mattie, her hands red from scrubbing, her eyes tired but sharp. The sound of her voice saying *cleanup*. He thought of War Eagle and String Bean hammering away at the ranch, of Adelina with that quiet steel in her spine. What a find for War Eagle. They were building something worth keeping.

And he was still out here, chasing ghosts, washing down salty beef with bitter water.

The night pressed close. He drifted somewhere between thought and sleep until the horse snorted—one sharp, warning sound.

Coble was awake before the second breath, gun drawn, eyes cutting toward the noise.

A figure stood at the edge of the wash, small and thin, backlit by moonlight. Not a man. A boy, maybe twelve, maybe less.

Coble kept his voice calm. "You lost, son?"

The boy shook his head, clutching something in his hands. "Got a message for you."

"A message? Who from?" Coble was finally coming awake. "How in hell did you find me?"

"Man said his name was Tibby and told me about where you'd be."

So he's watching.

Coble froze. It might as well have been Tibby standing there. He'd slept too sound. As if in agreement, an owl hooted in the distance.

"Go on," he said softly. "What's your message?"

The boy swallowed, his throat working like a trapped rabbit's. "He said...he said to tell you he has your woman."

The world narrowed to a pinpoint.

Coble's mind went white, not with rage, but with the cold, clean clarity that only comes when a man finally hits the edge of what he can stand.

He lowered the gun slowly. "Are you sure that's what he said?"

The boy nodded so fast it was almost a shiver. "He gave me this, too."

He held out a small scrap of fabric, blue cotton, torn uneven from a dress, stiff with a dark stain.

Coble didn't need to touch it to know it was real.

Mattie's. He'd taken that dress off her more than once.

He took the cloth and turned it over once in his palm. His hand trembled despite himself.

"Where'd you see him?"

The boy was trying to edge away.

"Near town. By the bridge. He said he was riding south come morning."

Coble's jaw tightened until his teeth hurt. "You ride straight home. Don't stop. If you see him again, tell him I got the message. But you ride slow, be careful."

The boy made a chuffing sound. "Mister, I was born out here." He hesitated, looking at the revolver, at Coble's shadowed face. "You're that marshal everyone talks about...you gonna kill him?"

Coble slid the gun back into its holster. "That's the plan."

The boy nodded once, then turned and disappeared into the darkness. He must have found his horse because hoofbeats faded into the night.

Coble sat there a long time, the fabric clutched in his hand, holding it to his face.

He could still smell her on it—soap...antiseptic, smoke.

He closed his eyes, took one long breath, and stood. Should have kept that kid as a guide.

BY DAWN, he was riding hard again, cutting north along the creek bed. The world had gone gray and flat, traveling the same trail he'd been on the day before. He was being too predictable, but had to chance it. He'd welcome an ambush just to get his hands on the man.

Every hoofbeat echoed like a drum in his chest. He didn't stop to rest the horse or himself.

When the first rooftops of Lamar came into sight, his heart sank.

Smoke.

Not from chimneys, but from fire.

He kicked the tired horse into a gallop, thundering through the outskirts, past the livery, past the silent telegraph office. The smell hit him, burning canvas, oil, scorched timber.

Mattie's clinic.

Half of the roof was gone. The windows were black mouths yawning against the dawn.

He leaped from the saddle before the horse stopped, hitting the ground running.

Inside, everything was chaos. Tables overturned,

the floor was slick with spilled tinctures and blood. The washbasin shattered. The line of drying bandages hung torn and swaying.

"Mattie?" he shouted. His voice echoed off the walls.

No answer.

Only the groan of the building settling.

He stepped deeper, gun drawn, scanning every corner. The cot where Amos had been was empty, sheets ripped away. The air was thick with the sharp bite of carbolic—and something worse.

Then he saw it.

On the table where she'd worked: a single scalpel driven deep into the wood. Another scrap of the same blue fabric wrapped the handle. And underneath, a note.

The mill. Noon. Come alone.

Coble's throat went dry. He had the crazy thought that if Tibby ran out of pointed objects, he'd never be able to leave a message.

He pulled the scalpel free, wiped it clean with the cloth, and slipped both into his vest. Then, he turned and walked out the door.

By the time he reached the street, townsfolk gathered, whispering behind hands. No one spoke to him.

They didn't have to.

He mounted his horse and rode toward the ridge. Hell with waiting until noon.

THE RIDE WAS PUNISHING under a white and pitiless sun. Sweat soaked his shirt, turning the dust on his skin to mud. The dun stumbled once and then steadied out. Taking the warning, Coble slowed the horse to a fast walk, wishing he had time to go to the ranch for a fresh mount.

He rode without rest, without food, the image of that burned clinic burned harder into his mind than the heat itself.

When he finally crested the hill above the old sawmill, it was near midday. The place looked different in sunlight, more frame than building now, casting short, mean shadows.

He stopped the horse behind a thicket of scrub and studied the scene.

The mill yard was quiet. Too quiet. A single horse stood tied near the fence, stamping nervously. No other movement.

But he knew Tibby was there. He could feel the electric stillness in the air before a fight, the moment the world seemed to hold its breath.

He dismounted, tied off the reins, and checked his guns. Six rounds each. It would be enough.

Starting forward, the dirt crunched under his boots, dry and loud. Each step felt deliberate, heavy, as though he were walking across plowed ground.

"Coble."

The voice came from inside, ragged, hoarse, but clear.

Tibby.

"You came," the outlaw called. "I was worried you'd gotten soft."

Coble didn't answer.

"You got a habit," Tibby went on, tone mock-casual. "Chasing things that don't wanna be caught.

Thought maybe you'd finally learned to stay home and build fences."

Coble moved closer, every sense sharpened to a point, and finally answered. "Where is she?"

A laugh answered him, dry, thin, like the crackle of burning sage. "She's fine. For now. I'm saving her for later."

"You might as well let her go, Tibby. There won't be a later. Not for you."

He could see Tibby's shadow inside now, moving just beyond the doorway. There was a hitch in his step. Still hurt. Still dangerous as a wounded wolf.

Coble stopped ten yards out. "You burned my ranch, Tibby. Shot Amos. Kidnapped Mattie."

"Quite the indictment. I killed another man in her office too. Don't forget that one." Tibby stepped into the light. The left side of his shirt was crusted with blood, his face gray with pain. But his eyes burned bright and mean. He held a revolver in his right hand and a piece of rope in the other.

"Oh, I'm not forgetting anything. You'll answer for all of that."

"Don't flatter yourself," Tibby said. "This ain't about your ranch or your woman. This is about you. About finishing what you started when you missed."

Coble's eyes flicked past him, to the far wall, where a dark shape moved slightly. Mattie. Tied to a beam, gagged but conscious.

"You should let her go," Coble said, voice low.

"Now, why would I do that?" Tibby sneered. "She's my insurance."

"You have me and don't need her."

"Oh, I will," Tibby said. "But not just yet. See, I

want you to see it first, how easy it is to lose everything you pretend you can protect."

He raised his gun.

Coble didn't move. Didn't flinch. His voice was steady. "You shoot her, Tibby, and I'll gut you like a pig."

Tibby grinned. "You still think this is about bullets? It ain't. It's about who breaks first."

He took a half step forward, breathing hard.

Coble's hand hovered near his holster. He didn't need to draw yet, not until the next breath, the next heartbeat.

For a moment, the world balanced on the edge of sound...a whisper, wind, waiting.

Then, from behind the mill, a faint rustle.

Tibby's eyes darted sideways.

Coble moved.

His revolver cleared leather in a single fluid motion. The first shot tore through Tibby's sleeve, spinning him. The second hit the post above his head.

Tibby fired back, wild, one round grazing Coble's shoulder.

Mattie screamed behind the gag.

Coble dove sideways behind a beam as the air filled with the roar of gunfire and splinters.

When the smoke cleared, Tibby was gone. Again.

The rope around Mattie's wrists hung loose, cut halfway through.

Coble ran to her, slashed the rest with his knife. "You all right?"

She nodded, voice hoarse. "He's...he's hurt bad. He can't go far."

"Where?"

"Ran out back. Toward the ridge." She gave him a stern look. "I'm going to have to give you shooting lessons."

Coble glanced once at the open door, sunlight spilling through the smoke.

He holstered his gun, jaw set like iron.

"This ends today," he said.

Chapter Twenty-Five

THEY HIT THE BACK DOORWAY TOGETHER. COBLE first, Mattie half a step behind, tossing away the gag he'd just cut free. Sunlight knifed across the mill yard. Tibby's tracks tore through dust and scrap toward the southeast, where the ground sloped away in low hills.

"Runaway Creek," Coble said. "If he's headed for that cabin, we've already burned it."

"How far is it?" Mattie gasped.

"Half a mile. Maybe less."

Coble shoved his knife back into the sheath and checked his revolver. Reloaded. He slid the cylinder shut with his thumb, the click was small and final.

"Can you ride? I don't want to leave you behind."

"I can," she said. "You won't lose me."

"That's something I never want to do. Never again."

He handed her his Winchester. "I'm sure you know how to use the rifle."

"I can handle it," she said, shouldering the rifle.

They cut around the mill and found Tibby's mount

blown and tied to a mesquite, reins tangled through the brush. Tibby had taken to foot. Blood marked the dirt in commas and smears. He was bleeding faster now. Coble cut the horse free with one swipe of his belt knife.

"We need to keep pushing him hard. Stay to my left," he told Mattie. "If he fires, he'll lead me and miss you."

"Don't tell me where to stand," she said. "Tell me where to shoot."

He didn't argue. They pushed into a canter, then a pounding run, the mill shrinking behind them into a dull, bad memory.

The ground here went from prairie grass to broken, brush-filled animal trails. Runaway Creek wasn't a creek most days, just a dry cut wandering toward distant river country, a place where the land was rough and uninviting. Cottonwoods marked the winding scar, their leaves stirring in a breeze that didn't touch the open flats. Beyond the trees, the earth sagged. Sinkhole country. Caverns ran underneath like hollow veins, and every season or two, the roof let go. You didn't ride fast in such places unless you wanted to be swallowed.

Tibby's trail slid off the wagon track and ghosted into tall grass. Coble slowed to a trot, eyes hunting for a sign. "He's cutting for the bend," he said.

"The sinkhole's there," Mattie said. "An old well collapsed into it. I stitched a drover who fell in once. He lived. Broke both legs and learned to pray."

"I'm surprised you know of that place."

A magpie hopped along a branch in the cottonwoods and scolded them. The horse beneath Coble tensed, ears flicking forward.

"Down," he said.

The shot came a breath later, flat and close. A puff of dust kicked up six inches in front of the sorrel's forefoot. Coble hauled the reins and slid out of the saddle on the far side, dragging Mattie by the knee with his free hand. They hit the dirt together, rolled behind a broken limestone hump. Another shot cracked, louder. Chips stung his cheek.

"Timberline, to the left," Mattie said, already bringing the Winchester up. She didn't shake or shout. She settled the sights like she meant to sew a line through the day.

Coble eased up for a glance. A flicker of a gray shirt appeared behind the cottonwood burl. Tibby's left side pressed to the trunk, right arm extended, pistol steady despite the tremor he couldn't hide. The man had patience, even bleeding. He'd taken ground that forced the approach into the open. The creek bed behind him, sinkhole past that. A bad man's geometry.

Coble counted silently: one shot, then another, then Tibby's breath. The pause was the truth.

"On my move," Coble said. "He'll shoot at me. You take the bark two inches above his wrist."

"I'll take the wrist," Mattie said.

He closed his eyes for one breath and remembered the sound of the barn burning, the taste of cinders, the empty place where good used to live. Then he rose, slow, hat first. Tibby fired. It was a reflex more than judgment, and the brim jumped, spun, and flew. Coble stood into the shot and put one round into the tree's edge, shaving bark, forcing a reaction.

Mattie's rifle spat.

Tibby yelped, not the high sound of surprise, but the lower sound men make when a joint goes wrong. His gun clattered into the scrub.

"Move," Coble said. He cut left, Mattie right, both angling to split Tibby's options.

The outlaw dove for the creek bed, faster than a wounded man ought to move. He hit the slope and slid in a half-crouch, a small avalanche of loose soil chasing him down. Coble followed to the lip and saw him pop up farther along, running hunched, left arm clamped to his ribs, right hand bloody and useless.

"Tibby," Coble called, voice hard as fence wire. "Give it up. You're done."

Tibby didn't answer. He cut across open ground toward the cottonwoods at the bend, where dark grass ringed a sag in the earth. Dragonflies skimmed the edges, riding the cool air rising from the earth.

"Sinkhole," Mattie said, coming up beside Coble. "Watch your feet. All this is hollow."

Coble stopped. "How do you know all this?"

"You were gone three years, Coble. Do you think I just lived at the clinic? Never rode the trails, saw the country? The girls and I liked to ride. Now, watch your feet."

He nodded and started down the bank, keeping low. The creek bed offered cover, a twisting, ribbed trough of clay and limestone. Here and there, deep pockets held last month's water, scabbed now with green scum. Mosquito country. The sun hammered the back of his neck.

Up ahead, Tibby glanced back, saw them, and veered toward a deadfall log fallen across the cut. He rolled over it, vanished, reappeared ten yards farther at a shallow ford. His gait had gone ragged, hips collapsing between strides. He was losing blood quickly.

Coble slid to a stop behind a snag and drew a breath. "Circle him," he told Mattie. "Get into that line of cottonwoods and keep him busy. I'll press him forward."

"You think he doesn't know where he is?"

"Oh, he knows," Coble said. "And he thinks we don't. It's the only play he has."

He looked at her then, really looked. Soot on her hairline. A nick of dried blood under her eye. The tightness in her jaw fighting whatever shook inside her. "Look, you don't have to—"

"I'm already in it," she said. "Go."

They broke apart. Coble followed the edge of the stream, staying low, moving when Tibby moved, freezing when Tibby looked back. Mattie kept to the high ground, weaving between cedar stumps and limestone knobs, angling her fire so any shot that went through would bury in clay.

Tibby reached the bend and swung around, desperate and bright-eyed. The ground trembled faintly under his heels. He saw Mattie first, maybe because the sight of her hurt his pride more than the pistol hurt his hand. He raised his gun with fingers that didn't want to work.

Mattie fired.

The bullet tore a furrow across Tibby's shoulder and spun him. He fired blindly...one ugly, lucky shot.

Mattie's breath jerked in. She staggered and went down hard into the knee-high bunchgrass.

Coble's body moved before thought caught up. He stood fully, reckless, and ran in a straight line along the creek bottom, boots thudding, breath roaring. Tibby saw him, swore, and fired again. The bullet stitched clay a foot from Coble's boot and ricocheted with a high wasp whine.

"Hey," Coble shouted, the word sharp as the crack of a whip. "Look at me, you son of a—"

Tibby looked.

Coble's running shot went low and hit Tibby in the thigh.

The outlaw crumpled, rolled, scrambled. He made the cottonwood line and grabbed for a root to pull himself up the short bank. The surrounding earth gave a little under his weight and didn't quite hold him. He froze, finally feeling the ground move beneath him.

The sinkhole yawned ahead, a dark oval the size of a barn floor, ringed with collapsed limestone and a fringe of cattails that had no business growing without water. A ruin of an old stone well leaned half-in, half-out along the near rim, its rockwork split and tilted, the mouth a crooked zero. Air seeped up cold from down there, smelling of damp rock and old, hidden places. A thin thread of sound rose too, water somewhere below, plodding, patient.

Coble came up the bank twenty feet to Tibby's right and held there, gun steady. He didn't fire. Not yet. Not with Mattie down. Not on this ground that might swallow them all as payment.

Tibby laughed once. His teeth were pink. "Well, hell," he said, breath hitching. "Look where we met after all. Bottom of the world."

"Step back from the rim," Coble said.

"Or what?" Tibby panted. "You'll shoot me and push me in? That doesn't sound like you. You like to see what you've killed. You like to put a name on it."

Coble didn't answer. He flicked his gaze left. Mattie was on one knee now, face white and focused, her left sleeve soaked dark near the biceps. She'd cinched it tight with her own kerchief. She saw him looking and nodded once: *I'm here*. Then she raised the Winchester again and settled it with a surgeon's care.

Tibby saw that nod. Saw the rifle level at him. Sneered. "Doc," he called, "you stitch me once and shoot me twice? That the oath?"

"One fracture at a time," Mattie said, voice thin but steady. "Put the gun down."

Tibby shifted his weight, and the ground answered. A hiss, a sigh, earth settling around a secret. The rim gave a handful of inches, then held.

"Leave it," Coble said, soft now, like talking to a spooked horse. "There's nowhere to run that isn't down."

"Down is where I was always going with you," Tibby said. He grinned quick and mean, as if meanness were the last coin he had to spend. "But I ain't going alone."

He jerked his arm and fired at Mattie.

Coble shot him in the forearm before the barrel cleared full of her. The impact knocked Tibby sideways. His pistol spun, skittered, and dropped into the hole, bouncing stone to stone in fading clinks that ended in a splash so far below it was hard to judge distance.

Silence strode in, bold as any man.

Coble moved first, two careful steps. "It's done," he said. "Back up."

Tibby's face shifted. The light in it went from bright to flat, the look men get when they finally count up their time left. He looked at his hand, at the slick red cuff of his shirt. And looked at Mattie, set there like a line he couldn't cross. He looked into the sinkhole. The gasp of breath he drew sounded like it hurt.

"So, you think you've won," he said conversationally. "You never understood me. You think I lit barns 'cause I like the glow. I did it 'cause people run toward fire. You all run toward it. You can't help yourselves."

"Step back," Coble said.

Tibby shook his head. Small, almost gentle. "No. I think I'll let the ground choose."

He rocked his weight to stand. The rim slumped an inch. The old well groaned. A hairline crack chased itself around the circle. Coble felt it through his boots, up his shins, into his teeth.

"Don't," Coble said, and surprised himself with the word. It wasn't mercy. It was a refusal to let chance take what work and will had earned. "You look at me when you go."

Tibby did. For the first time in all the scrapes and sprints and smoke, he really looked, and the grin died. Some recognition moved in him, maybe of the road behind, maybe of the shape of what he'd made. He swallowed. Blood ran down his chin. "Say my name," he said, defiant to the last. "Say it so it sticks."

Coble's jaw set. "Tibby," he said, as if writing a verdict. "This is where you end."

"Hell," Tibby whispered, and took a half step back.

The ground gave.

It didn't roar. It sighed. The rim slumped as a piece and folded inward. The cattails toppled like gangly men, the old well's circle split into two drunk halves and slid. Dust lifted in a smooth, horrible curtain. The center opened and drew everything toward itself with a lazy hunger.

Instinctively, Tibby scrabbled for purchase. His right boot found the broken edge of the well ring and held. His fingers clawed at the loose dirt. For a breath, he hung there, every tendon in his neck standing out, eyes wild and animal.

Coble moved without thinking. He holstered his gun, dropped to his belly, and reached. The ground between them lipped and crumbled. He could feel the hollowness under his chest, the emptiness humming.

"Take my hand," he said. Fury burned through him. Not mercy, not pity...ownership. The ending belonged to him, not to a hole.

Tibby's eyes cut to the hand. Should he take it? He could come up, spit blood, and end standing, maybe meet the bullet he deserved.

He smiled that small, thin smile that had ruined so many days. "Go to hell," he echoed, and let go.

Disappearing fast and quiet, his figure fell through light into the throat of the earth. Dust swirled over the opening. Stones clicked and slid. Then the noise changed, less crumble, more echo. A far-off splash rang up the shaft, faint as a memory.

The ground settled by degrees. The inward pull eased as the rim found a new, uglier circle and held.

Coble lay there a breath longer, hand still out, rage

cooling to a gray slab inside his chest. He breathed. It tasted like limestone and old water.

"Coble." Mattie's voice was thin. Not frightened. Present.

He pushed to his knees and went to her, moving carefully across ground that had just changed its mind. Up close, he saw the wound, through-and-through along the outside of the upper arm, meat torn, bleeding steady but not pumping. He tore his bandana, twisted it above the hole, and tied it off. She didn't flinch. Sweat slicked her temple. Her eyes were bright and far away, the place a person goes when they decide to stay.

"Hurts," she said. It wasn't a complaint.

"Good," he said gently, digging for the little dig she'd given him at the clinic. He found it. "Means there's enough of you to feel it."

He packed clean cloth, at least what he had, and bound it tight. The bleeding slowed. He kept one hand on the knot a little longer than necessary, feeling the heat of her skin, the pulse stubborn under his thumb.

"Do you feel cheated? Because he chose the hole?"

He looked past her at the sinkhole. It sat muttering to itself, tiny sloughs of loose soil still giving way at the edges, leaves and sticks riding the wave. The cottonwoods leaned like curious men.

"Somewhat."

"Did you want to save him?" Her voice was soft, barely heard over the wind through the trees.

Surprised by the space the question opened, he pictured Tibby's hand in his, the pull, the kick of the earth, imagined the weight of those fingers. He turned the thought over and set it down.

"Save him? No," he said. "I wanted to kill him."

"That's honest," she said.

He sat back on his heels and drew a long breath that read the ledger of his body from teeth to boot heel. Something in his shoulder ached where the graze had dug a line. He pressed it once and let it go.

Behind them, the magpie fluttered to the rim and peered down, head cocked. It made a few bright, rude sounds, as if the whole affair had been for its amusement.

Mattie followed the bird with her eyes and then looked at him. "Help me stand."

He slid an arm around her back carefully and lifted. She was light as a coat rack until her boots were under her, and then she weighed exactly as much as the world. She swayed. He steadied her. She leaned a fraction longer than balance required, then set her jaw.

"Clinic first," he said. "To get you fixed up. Then sheriff, judge, any man who owns a pen. They should all know about Tibby. He'll get his fame."

He nodded toward the hole. "We'll show them where he lies."

"Do you need to do that?" she asked.

He didn't answer at once, watching the dust settle and the green of the cattails find their new angle. He listened to the trickle far below, where Tibby had gone to drown with his bad decisions.

"No," he said finally. "I don't need it. But the town does."

THEY MADE their way back along the creek bed to safer ground. The horse had wandered into the shade and looked offended to be reclaimed. Coble boosted Mattie up, she bit the inside of her cheek and said nothing. He mounted and took the reins of Tibby's played-out horse, because even a killer's beast deserved a clean stall and rest.

They talked little on the ride. The sun leaned west and went red at the edges, a second chance at dawn, if you were willing to lie to yourself. Wind came off the flats with grit in it. When the clinic's broken roofline appeared, Mattie made a small sound, part laugh, part curse. It wasn't home, but it was the door she walked through to keep men alive. That made it special enough.

On the street, two men looked up from a water barrel and froze. Springer's badge gleamed at the far end of the boardwalk, pinned to the man's vest again like a borrowed virtue. He squinted into the light and took one step toward them, then thought better of it.

Coble swung down and lifted Mattie in his arms. She allowed it for two steps and then insisted he plant her on her feet. He honored that with a steadying hand and the angled body of a man ready to catch pride before it broke.

Inside, the clinic smelled of ash and charred wood. He set her at the one table still fit to bear weight. She unrolled instruments that had no right to be clean and made them ready. He stood by until she looked up and said, "You going to hover or fetch water?"

He fetched water.

While she worked, one-handed, clever, and uncomplaining, he took the scalpel he'd pocketed and drove it point-down into the tabletop, not in anger but as a nail for a memory. The blue scrap beside it darkened with the last of Tibby's usefulness.

Mattie glanced at the blade, then at him. "You'll write it all up?"

"Every line," he said. "How he came. How he took you and how the ground took him back."

"And what about you?" she asked.

He touched the badge on his vest. It sat there like a truth reclaimed. "I'll hang this where it belongs," he said. "On a nail, for when somebody needs it. Not for polishing."

From the doorway came a throat being cleared, weak and theatrical. Springer stood there, hat in hand, "I—" he began.

"Don't," Coble said without turning. "Not now."

Springer swallowed, nodded, and disappeared the way he came.

Coble washed blood from his hands in a tin basin. The water went pink and swirled down a drain that splashed outside. He dried his fingers on a clean corner of a towel that Mattie had saved from the fire's teeth and looked at her stitching. Quick, confident bites into her own flesh.

"Hurts," she said again, like a benediction this time.

He nodded. "Good."

"If you say it a third time, it's a superstition," she warned.

He smiled. It surprised him how easily it came. "Then here's another. I'm taking you to the ranch when you're bandaged. War Eagle will growl. String Bean will boast. Adelina will fix a great meal for us."

"She will," Mattie said, very sure. "And you'll sit on that porch you rebuilt and feel the boards hold."

He looked out the window at the slanting light and the slow dust. The town breathed differently already—like a fever broken.

"Maybe," he said.

The room quieted. Somewhere, a freight whistle moaned far off, the rails carrying the vibration.

Mattie tied the last knot, bit the thread, and sat back. "How do you feel?"

"Tired," he said.

"That's honest," she judged. "I'll take it."

He picked up his hat from the chair where he'd dropped it and thumbed a crease back into the ragged brim. The bullet line in the felt would stay. Some marks you don't fix. You let them remind you.

Coble held out his hand for hers. "Let's go home."

They stepped into the evening together. The sky was long red streaks, leaning toward purple. People watched from porches and behind curtains, then stepped out, small clusters forming as they passed. No one cheered. This wasn't that kind of place, and Coble wasn't that kind of man.

But heads dipped in greeting. Hands touched brims in respect. A girl with a ribbon too bright for the dust smiled outright at Mattie, who lifted her chin, winked, and smiled back like a dare.

Coble took the reins and walked the horses toward the edge of town. Behind them, the clinic stood crooked and stubborn. Ahead, the road unrolled into the kind of distance that only ends when you stop.

By the time the sun slid under the world, the heat had eased, and a night wind came rolling off the prairie. It smelled of sage and creosote and the rumbling storm, far off.

At the ridge above Runaway Creek, they paused and looked down. The cottonwoods at the bend seemed to rustle and whisper in the wind. The sinkhole was just a dark circle in a brush-choked valley. No sound rose from it now. The evil it consumed slaked the earth's hunger.

"Go on," Mattie said. "Look as long as you need."

He did not need long. He tipped his hat to the ghosts and shadows that lived in the dark places and turned the horses toward home.

Chapter Twenty-Six

October started with a cold snap that set the mornings sharp as flint and painted the maples along Runaway Creek in fire. Frost silvered the pasture grass, and the air held a clean, brittle edge with a promise of winter close behind. The creek had dropped to a respectable level, no longer a swollen threat but a steady ribbon of clear water winding through the valley, murmuring across limestone ledges and rock.

The pens around the barn were a mess of noise and life, goats bleating, chickens fussing and scratching, and a half-grown hog that made a habit of escaping its pen just to be chased back in again by the two English shepherds that patrolled the barnyard and corrals. They were chest-deep with pride, barking at anything that moved faster than they did.

String Bean had traded with a German farmer over near Sutton Town for a few milk cows and, occasionally, the loan of his Angus-mix bull—a gentle creature so wide he carried shade for cowbirds and the occasional turkey.

Adelina's kitchen smelled of black coffee strong enough to float a horseshoe and warm bread. The big pine table doubled as their meeting place. Coble, Mattie, War Eagle, Adelina, and String Bean, all in their usual seats by some unspoken order. The windows fogged from the contrast of warm air and cold glass, and outside, mist rolled off the creek, hugging the low ground.

"Adelina," Coble said, setting down his cup. "I'm sorry, but you need to be fired."

The words dropped like a hammer. War Eagle, halfway through a swallow, choked and slammed his mug down. "What?"

Adelina raised one dark eyebrow, amusement already twitching at her mouth. Mattie snorted into her coffee, half trying not to, and cut a glance at Coble.

Coble leaned back, not bothered by the drama he'd caused. "Look around. There's a ton of work to be done, and look at War Eagle. I swear he's gained ten pounds since the first frost. If this keeps up, he'll need a pulley system to get in the saddle."

Laughing, Adelina poured more coffee into his cup, then War Eagle's. "I think John is shaping up nicely. He looked starving when we met."

Coble grinned. "John?" He glanced sideways at War Eagle, who went crimson from neck to hairline.

"I—uh—" War Eagle started.

Coble raised his palm. "Save it. *John*. We've got business."

String Bean looked up from his butter-slavered biscuit, wary. "Business? We got everything running slicker'n a greased pig. Thanks to me, naturally."

Coble reached into his coat, pulled out two brown envelopes, and slid them across the table toward War Eagle and String Bean. "Papers came yesterday. Both of you are now the new owners of the ranch. You get all the bills and headaches."

The room went still except for the wind scraping the shutters. Adelina froze mid-pour. Mattie blinked, and the dogs outside paused their racket, looking at the house.

Coble leaned back, smiling softly. "I figure you'll come up with a good name for it. Or them. You could split it in two."

Mattie's eyes narrowed slightly—suspicion mixed with surprise. He gave her a reassuring nod.

"I think *John*,"—Coble couldn't resist the emphasis—"needs to make whatever's going on with Adelina official. You two will need a home of your own."

Mattie smirked. "And a nursery."

Adelina groaned, hiding her face in her hands. "Mattie...not now."

But Coble kept going. "And as for String Bean. It's come to my attention he's been courting a certain widow down south. A fine woman. Runs a tidy farm, a small herd, four little ones, and the patience of a saint."

Mattie burst out laughing. "Sarah Ortiz? Oh, my God. I delivered her last baby. She's strong enough to whip a man with one hand and keep plowing with the other."

String Bean rolled his eyes, muttering something about *folks mindin' their own fences*.

Mattie grinned. "Official or not, she's already decided. He snuck through her window once, since she didn't shoot him, that's as good as a proposal in most towns."

String Bean groaned. "Can we please stop talkin' like I ain't here?"

War Eagle cleared his throat, still red but sincere. "Coble, that's too generous. We don't deserve this."

Coble shook his head. "Of course you do. You built this place back from ash and knee-deep mud, while I was chasing my tail looking for Tibby. Besides, the judge took it over for taxes and then gave it back to me. Now I'm giving it to the people who earned it. If he ever comes knockin' again"—he paused, eyes gleaming—"you can tell him to go ask Runaway Creek where the secrets are buried."

String Bean chuckled darkly. "Judges disappear every day."

"Not if they pay their taxes," Mattie quipped, sipping her coffee.

Coble pushed his chair back. "It's settled. The place is yours. I reckon it'll thrive better in your hands than mine."

He looked toward Mattie, who was already watching him with quiet suspicion. "Which brings me to my next bit of business. I'm inviting Miss Hurst to ride with me to Lamar today. We have...things to discuss."

War Eagle leaned forward, grinning. "I think we should go too. I still don't trust that town."

"Yes," Adelina nearly shouted. "We're low on air tights, and I need some...uh...personal items."

Coble sighed, raising both hands in mock surrender. "Fine. Let's make a parade of it."

———

By midmorning, the wagon and two horses rolled into Lamar under a deep blue sky. The autumn air was crisp, and smoke from dozens of chimneys hung low like soft gray ropes over Main Street. The storefronts gleamed with fresh paint—the town looked new somehow, with people making a fresh start.

Coble drew rein in front of the mercantile. "All right," he said, "y'all do your shoppin'. Meet me at the café across from the courthouse at noon."

The only response he got was Adelina laughing as she dragged War Eagle toward the fabric shop, and String Bean disappearing at an unnatural pace down the street, probably south toward Sarah Ortiz's sister's house. Sarah must be in town.

Mattie stayed where she was, reins loose in her hands.

"Might I ask where you're taking me?" she said, eyes suspicious but warm.

"You might," he said. "But that don't mean I'll answer."

She rolled her eyes as he guided their horses down a side street just off Main. They passed a new livery, with the sound of hammering echoing down the alley. Then, before her eyes, the whitewashed building appeared.

It stood fresh and proud, trimmed in forest green, windows shining like clear river glass. Over the front door hung a new sign: *LAMAR CLINIC*.

Mattie gasped, hand to her chest. "Coble..."

"It's yours," he said simply.

For a long moment, she couldn't move. Then she

slid off her horse and stepped inside, slow and reverent as if entering a church. The place smelled of oil soap and lacquer, the air moved curtains from open windows. She touched the polished counter, the sanded cabinets, and ran her fingers across the smooth surface of an exam table.

"These will be easy to clean," she murmured.

Four rooms stretched behind the waiting area, exam spaces, a small dispensary, and even a back entrance shaded by a poplar tree. She turned back to him, eyes glassy.

"You did this for me?"

He nodded. "Had some help. You're a healer, Mattie. Always have been. Out at the ranch, you were fading—too much waiting, not enough doing. This... this is what you were made for."

Her eyes filled, chin raised stubbornly. "I can't. Not like this."

That caught him. "I don't understand?"

"I don't want us to be apart again," she said softly.

Coble chuckled, shaking his head. "Weren't you listening at breakfast? I don't have a ranch anymore. Sold my stake—gave it, really. What I do have is a house one street over. Not big, but close enough I can smell your coffee if the wind's right."

The words hit her harder than she'd expected. "Coble Bray, are you telling me—"

Before she could finish, a door opened in the back. Two familiar voices echoed down the hall, followed by laughter.

Mattie gasped again as Joanne and Amos stepped into the room. "You two—?"

Amos grinned, wearing a vest that looked suspiciously official. Joanne, wiping her hands, smiled wide. "Surprise. Amos built half your shelves, and I talked Coble into letting me be your assistant. Figure I've already mopped up enough blood in my time to handle yours."

Mattie turned, overwhelmed. "But Coble...this won't make money right away, not until I stock—"

He stepped closer, his smile gentler now. "Don't worry about that."

Her eyes narrowed. "What did you do?"

He hesitated just long enough to make her suspicious. "Well, the county sheriff decided to retire. And the town constable went with him."

"I didn't know there was a town constable." Mattie's shoulders sagged. "So you're taking the badge again?"

He grinned and pulled his coat aside. A new badge gleamed there, smaller, polished, marked simply Town Constable.

"Not that badge," he said. "This new one means I sleep at home every night. Mostly. And I've even got a deputy."

Mattie turned toward Amos, who was suddenly studying the floorboards like they held the secret to eternity. A badge shone on his vest.

"You?" she said.

Amos looked up, sheepish. "Couldn't let him get shot alone."

Mattie sank into a chair, laughter and tears mixing. "I don't even know what to say."

Joanne crossed her arms, smirking. "Say yes, dummy."

"Excuse me?"

Joanne laughed outright. "Because that big oaf's about to ask you to marry him, if he can ever spit it out."

Mattie blinked, then turned to Coble. "Are you?"

He nodded. "Please."

She smiled through tears. "Okay, then. Yes."

"Well, that was easy enough."

Joanne rolled her eyes.

He pulled her into a hug that smelled of cedar and lavender, and the long trail finally ended. "Just think," he murmured, "maybe the justice of the peace can do three weddings."

Mattie laughed into his chest. "Oh no, just two. Sarah Ortiz will have a proper Catholic wedding, with half the county invited. String Bean won't know what hit him."

"Serves him right," Joanne said, still grinning. "It's about time he got domesticated."

Coble kissed the top of Mattie's head. "You realize we're about to have an entire generation of screaming kids between the ranch and that farm?"

Mattie looked up at him, smiling. "Good. This land needs some happiness."

THAT EVENING, the sun bled out slowly across the hills. Smoke from the chimneys curled in steady blue trails over Lamar. Wagons hauling firewood would roll all fall and winter. In the distance, Runaway Creek murmured softly, tamed now after a season of storms.

Coble stood on the small porch of their new house, four rooms, fresh paint, a little yard out front. Behind him, Mattie was unpacking jars and linens, humming under her breath. From somewhere down the street came laughter, children chasing a stray chicken. The world, for once, was simple.

He pulled his old marshal's badge from his pocket and turned it in his palm, the metal worn smooth by time and use. Finally, he returned it to his pocket. It had a date with Runaway Creek the next time he went that way. When he turned, Mattie was watching from the porch.

"Can you let it go?" she asked. "Every problem you've ever had was solved with a lead ball or walking away. Can you do it this time?"

He realized she was right. Thinking back through the years, and more recently with the killer in Hard Times, of the Pianoman, and Tibby—his life had been centered around killers of men whose redemption came with a lead ball. Could he change?

"I think it's time." He nodded. "Finally."

She smiled. "Good. Come inside before supper gets cold."

He followed her in, closing the door softly behind him. The house smelled of bread and wood smoke, the faint trace of linseed oil from her hands. She'd been working on furniture.

Coble glanced at her across the small table, her hair catching the lamplight, her smile easy and sure. The world was still full of mystery, but for the first time in years, he didn't feel the need to chase them.

Chapter Twenty-Seven

The first snow came early.

A thin, hesitant dusting drifted down from a heavy sky, landing in the furrows of the ranch yard and on the backs of the English shepherds. By sundown, the flakes thickened, falling straight and soft.

War Eagle Parker—John now, though Coble was the only man alive brave enough to say it—stood at the top of the ridge, coat open, letting the cold settle into him. The ranch below looked calm, fences mended, roofs tight, smoke rising steadily from the chimney of the ranch house. Inside, he could see the halo of lamplight, the shape of Adelina moving from stove to table.

He closed his eyes. A man could get used to this, a quiet that didn't come with fear, a life that didn't need a gun hanging over it like a shadow. He'd lived that life a long time. If Coble could change, so could he.

He heard hoofbeats shuffling in the snow and didn't turn. "You ride too quiet for a big man," he said.

String Bean snorted. "Ain't my fault you stand

around broodin' like a church gargoyle." His horse chuffed beside him, breath fogging the air. "Storm's coming. You staying out here till you freeze solid?"

"What the hell is a ...? Never mind. I'm just looking the place over," War Eagle said.

"Mm." String Bean followed his gaze. "You think she'll say yes?"

War Eagle's jaw tightened. "You mind your own courtin'. How is Sarah, by the way? We have lots of room at the house for y'all to move in."

String Bean blushed instantly, an impressive feat for a brown man half-frozen. "She's...well." He scratched the back of his neck. "The kids like me. Even the baby. She hasn't thrown me out yet."

"High praise," War Eagle murmured.

"Shut up."

They stayed quiet awhile, watching the snow settle on fence rails and barn roofs, the world softening under winter's first blanket. Finally, String Bean cleared his throat.

"You ever think about how close we came?" he asked. "Losing it all?"

War Eagle didn't answer right away. He thought of Tibby, the fires, the gunfights, the sinkhole at Runaway Creek swallowing truth after truth until there wasn't much left to fear.

"Yes," he said finally. "I have been, but I'm done looking backward."

Satisfied, String Bean nodded. "Me too." Then he smiled. "Mostly."

Down in Lamar, the lanterns on Main Street were lit one by one as dusk rolled in. It was too cold for the kids to pester the lamplighter on stilts. Coble Bray walked the length of the street, checking doors that should be locked, boots crunching in the fresh snow. The evening was quiet except for the distant sound of a piano drifting from the saloon, a slow tune, nothing rowdy. Since he'd talked them into closing at midnight, things had changed.

This was a family town, not a wide-open boom town. Folks had settled since Tibby and the useless county sheriff departed—one buried deep, the other seeking greener pastures.

He wore the constable's badge under his coat now, not on the outside. Lamar didn't need the shine of authority as much as it needed the certainty of it, and Coble had found peace in being a lawman whose job was less shooting and more steady presence.

He paused outside the Lamar Clinic. Light spilled from the windows, golden and warm. Inside, Mattie worked late, not because of injury or illness, but because she enjoyed tending to her people. The waiting room was empty, except for a pot of peppermint tea and a knitted blanket someone's grandmother had left as thanks. Exam tables were shiny clean, and the shelves were full. Mattie always waited patiently for him to do his rounds every evening.

Coble stepped in quietly. Mattie looked up from her ledger, a smile warming her eyes. "Cold out there?"

"Not so much," Coble said. "Storm's moving in slow."

She walked over, looping her arm through his. "Everything quiet tonight?"

He nodded. "Quiet as a church at noon."

"Quiet." Mattie rested her head briefly on his shoulder. "I like that."

He did too.

"Joanne coming in to help tomorrow?" he asked.

"She is," Mattie said, returning to her desk, closing the ledger. "Amos is bringing by a man with a busted ankle. Claims he fell off a ladder. Amos says the ladder claims it was pushed."

Coble chuckled. "Best let 'em both tell their stories."

"That's working out, you know," she said. "Using Amos to go get patients who are hurt to bring them in. It was a good idea."

He shrugged. "Even a blind hog finds an acorn once in a while."

Mattie watched him as he shed his coat and hung it by the stove. "Coble?"

"Yes, ma'am?"

"Are you okay? Really okay?"

"You keep asking me that." He nodded once, slow. "I am."

She shrugged. "There's a lot of gun smoke in your past. I'd think it would be hard to slow down."

"I didn't say it was easy. You're a big help."

Apparently that was the right thing to say, since she slipped into his arms. For the first time since he'd come to this town, Coble felt the land settle around him like a blanket rather than a burden.

Mattie smiled. "Good. Now, we need to get home because Amos is coming to supper. I need you to keep him from eating the pie before the rest of us get a slice."

Coble shook his head. "Ain't no badge in the world that gives me that kind of authority."

"What happened to his woman?" he continued.

"Unknown." She winked. "Joanne's kinda steppin' in."

He gazed at her for a moment until she shrugged.

"Don't ask, don't tell?" he asked.

"It's a new world." She nudged him with her hip.

"Lost souls, and all that?"

Mattie laughed, a soft, warm sound he never tired of.

The world was changing.

He had to change with it, or he stood to lose more than just his soul.

Runaway Creek murmured in the distance, carrying winter's icy whisper. No ghosts in it now. No bones. Just water sliding toward spring.

A Look at Osage Dawn:
By Darrel Sparkman

Amid the dust and blood of conflict, there lies a deeper truth.

On the northern Arkansas border of 1804, an Osage warrior and a young trapper pit wits and strength in a deadly battle only one will survive.

When Matt Crane left home to travel the far western lands, he didn't intend to be gone long. Four years later, he returns to find his family dead, his hometown destroyed, and his sweetheart taken captive by Quick Killer, a vicious renegade Osage warrior with a score to settle.

Kidnapping the woman Matt loves is only the beginning of Quick Killer's plan as he seeks revenge upon Matt, the architect of his shame. What he fails to realize, though, is that he faces an adversary far more tenacious than he ever thought possible—one that will push his very limits.

In a showdown that will test their resolve and redefine their fates, Matt Crane and Quick Killer must confront their deepest fears and come to terms with the legacy of their actions—and the ties that bind them.

A fast-paced frontier adventure, Osage Dawn *blends love and raw adventure in the wild frontier, where history was made amid gut-wrenching fights for survival.*

AVAILABLE NOW

About the Author

Darrel Sparkman is an award-winning author of novels, novellas, and short stories. He's been included in three western anthologies, worked as a feature writer for *Saddlebag Dispatches* and blogged a short time for *Sundown Press*.

His ideas come from a diverse past of serving as a combat search and rescue helicopter crewman in Vietnam and volunteer Emergency Medical Technician First Responder. He has worked as a professional photographer, computer repair tech, and was once part-owner of a commercial greenhouse operation and flower shop.

Darrel is enjoying semi-retirement and finally has that job that wakes him up every day—with a smile on his face.

www.ingramcontent.com/pod-product-compliance
Lightning Source LLC
La Vergne TN
LVHW040217110826
845146LV00005B/1320

* 9 7 9 8 8 9 5 6 7 4 6 8 0 *